In

One hot summer weekend in July, something odd is about to happen at the old tavern. The whole village is getting ready for fun and celebration at the annual Independence Festival weekend down by the river, in one of the oldest parts of town, when space and time collide.

Something has gone missing. Or has it? Maryvonne has set up her easel across from the old tavern early one morning when she is visited by early American novelist Tabitha Gilman Tenney, and begins to learn about some of the contributions of the Revolutionary War era Black community in Exeter, New Hampshire.

Exeter Green Press | Exeter, New Hampshire
2022

Second Edition December 2021
Original Publication January 2020

Many names of places and people are fictitious,
some are not.

Exeter Green Press
Exeter, New Hampshire
ExeterNhArts.com
ISBN-13: 978-0-9883744-5-4

Author's Note

I never intended to write a trilogy. However, this first book was so well received by the town that my husband encouraged me to write more books. It also helped that it was the long winter of the pandemic lockdown.

This book was written as a means to an end: to help make more visible the previously neglected history and contributions of the historic Black community in Exeter. Since the original publication in 2019 the townsfolk of Exeter have rallied. There are now at least five public, tangible elements in the town that honor that old community. And several more on the way, possibly including a pocket park.

The time is right now to do some small updates to the original first book. Welcome to the second edition of Incident at Exeter Tavern (set in Revolutionary War-era Exeter). The cover and "Historical Facts" page now match the other two books in the series: Incident at Ioka (set in Abolitionist-era Exeter) and Incident at Exeter Depot (set in Suffragette-era Exeter). And in an exciting twist, this book has set people sleuthing through databases and because of their efforts, I am able to update the book with historical details on the Hall family saga. But the mystery of young James still remains unsolved.

Persist sleuths! May my books prompt questions only you can track down and answer. Then celebrate your findings and send them to the Exeter Historical Society for their files.

May my cozy-capers inspire you to ponder what could have been. May they inspire graciousness toward all.

RM Allen, December 2021

In memory of
Rhoda (Paul) Hall
1769 - 1844

Special thanks to
Exeter Historical Society
David Weber
Lew Hitzrot

Old Historical Facts

- Revolutionary War soldier Jude Hall, his signature above, lived and died as described in this book
- A memorial stone was erected for him in 2001, near to the lost original
- "Jude's Pond" still appears on Exeter, NH maps
- Rhoda Hall's testimony appeared in the Liberator newspaper in 1834

New Historical Facts

- Members of Exeter's community of Black Revolutionary War veterans will be honored with prominent historical signage in 2022
- The Black Heritage Trail of NH will collaborate with Exeter on a project soon
- The "Jude & Rhoda Hall Society" was created in 2021, after the family tree was researched
- The descendants are many, and live both regionally and nationally
- The American Independence Museum's educational collection now contains the 2021 painting "Jude Hall at the Powder House" (inset above)

CONTENTS

(Thanks to Jimi Hendrix for these song titles)

Chapter 1

All along the watchtower…
Two riders were approaching and the wind began to howl

Almost a week ago, Maryvonne came face-to-face with the airbag in her car during a fender-bender in the parking lot at the entrance to the market. A distracted driver ran a stop sign and plowed right into her little hybrid car. This was a minor accident resulting in a small purple bump, and lingering headaches.

The doctor advised Maryvonne that she had a concussion and should rest inside in a darkened room for a few days. Little did she know while she was resting how odd things were about to get: cue the spangles.

Today she was feeling much better and wanted to get out; the weather was glorious. It had been a cold, wet and disappointing spring and early summer, but an excellent July so far. When she stepped outside early this morning to test the temperature, she felt the warm promise of this new day and smiled. The balmy air made her head feel much better. It was time to get back to her life and commitments.

She had agreed to submit a painting this Saturday to an art auction on Sunday. Today was Thursday, and time was running out. Returning inside the house she moved quickly through the quiet kitchen, fed the dog, and gathered her supplies. When she stepped back outside, Maryvonne packed her French easel and a blank canvas into her husband's little blue Miata convertible, affectionately known as the Zeus-mobile, and turned left onto High Street towards downtown Exeter, New Hampshire.

It was fifteen minutes past five when she saw Joe Saints Coffeeshop and Bakery coming up in the distance. A slender woman in white leggings with hair in long cornrows was running across the street in front of the shop, holding something large and flat behind her in an odd way. Maryvonne was too far away to see it clearly, but it appeared to possibly be a large cork board or whiteboard. Just as she got almost close enough to see, the woman slipped into the space in between Joe Saints and the white colonial building next door which housed the summer school office of the local prep school. Pulling into the parking lot behind Joe Saints and the summer office, she gave a quick look around to see if the woman was still there. But she was not.

Maryvonne got out of the car and carried her art gear to the front sidewalk. Thankfully, it was so early that she had the street all to herself. She decided she would set up the easel, quickly sketch out her scene, choose her colors, then get hot coffee at 6am when Joe Saints opened. Then happily nurse that coffee all morning until the painting was complete.

The Exeter-Folsom Tavern was to be her subject. It stood directly across from the coffee shop. She set up her easel one door down from the coffee shop, outside an office building with a large glass front and a mod overhang supported by large, square, cement columns. She would paint from under the shade of a small ornamental fruit tree that stood at the entrance.

The building had been recently sold and was still unoccupied, which made the spot all the more perfect. From that angle she was able to get a good view of the sweep of the tavern's front facade as well as a portion of the side yard and its bushes and trees.

Her site all set to go, she did what she usually did next, which was to put in her purple earbuds to get motivated by some music stored on her MP3 player. And as a bonus, she found people left her alone when they saw she had earphones in her ears. That was the point of the highly noticeable bright purple strings. She usually listened to music while painting plein-air; it wiped all distractions away and helped her to get her head into a creative cocoon, focusing her thoughts into "the flow" of painting her subject.

In the morning sun, Maryvonne brushed her blonde shoulder-length hair aside and hit Play just in time to hear Jimi say, "There must be some kind of way outta here, said the joker to the thief..." The funky beat was thumping inside her head in manic competition with her suddenly slightly throbbing headache.

All the movement of getting there and setting up her gear must have proved a bit too much action for her tender head. "Oh la la," she groaned. This was not going to work.

Right now in the morning sun, Jimi's amped-up electric guitar was wailing in a way that usually tingled her right down to her toes, but not today. There was a feeling in her head, but it had a different shape than the tingle – and also a bit of undulating light? Maybe like a jarring spangle? Odd, but fleeting. Grimacing, she hoped that tomorrow or the next day her head would be back to normal.

"Sorry Jimi, my friend, maybe later," she groaned aloud as she slipped the purple earbuds out, hoping hot coffee would help smooth out the frazzled edges. She checked her watch: twenty-five minutes until Joe Saints opened. She took a deep breath.

Focusing with painter's eyes, she now looked across the street at the house she would be rendering on the canvas. The historic Folsom Tavern was a small wooden Colonial-style house that had entertained George Washington just after the Revolutionary War when Exeter was the official financial capital of New Hampshire.

It was a naturally-aged brown wooden home, with mustard yellow trim, old fashioned "12 over 12" pane windows, and two big chimneys, also painted mustard. "Hmm, moutarde," Maryvonne wrinkled her nose at the color, pronouncing it in proper French under her breath.

Behind it and up on a small hill held fast by an old stone wall sat its partner home, the much larger Ladd-

Gilman House. Both buildings were owned by the same non-profit entity, the American Independence Museum. The two were connected by a long, looping, nicely landscaped path that curved its way over the hill past benches, bushes, sculptures, and informational placards.

This was Maryvonne's first time seeing the new path whole since its completion earlier in the spring. She had read in the newspaper that the new path told a story as you journeyed along between the two historic buildings; it was a story-path.

The Ladd-Gilman building was a soft yellow Colonial with white trim and black shutters. The many visitors were pleased to find out that it was three buildings in one - it just kept going on down the line, like an ornately beaded necklace, with room additions and gables and porches on both sides. A plaque on the front read "Ladd-Gilman House 1721." This well-kept historic building had hosted the 1776 New Hampshire State Treasury run by the treasurer Nicholas Gilman Jr.

The townspeople were proud of the history of this yellow house and the story was well-known. Nicholas Jr. was a soldier in the Continental Army during the American Revolutionary War, a delegate to the Continental Congress, and a signer of the U.S. Constitution, representing New Hampshire. He was a member of the United States House of Representatives during the first four Congresses, and served in the U.S. Senate from 1805 until his death in 1814. His younger brother John Taylor Gilman, also a patriot and politician, would go on to become governor of New Hampshire for fourteen years. This was their childhood home, but not the only Gilman house in town. Gilman was the big name in Exeter, so there were Gilmans aplenty both then and now.

The museum owned an original copy of the Declaration of Independence, commonly called a Dunlap Broadside. They were created to spread the word in 1776 about the document that Thomas Jefferson, Benjamin Franklin and the other founding fathers had just finalized. They had two hundred "broadsides," or large, single-sided, copies printed on the evening of July 4th 1776 by Philadelphia printer John Dunlap. These complete copies of the Declaration of Independence, word-for-word but unsigned, were sent by horseback to the thirteen colonies and various other important entities.

Only twenty-six of these broadside-style copies still remain - and they are quite valuable. And rather tempting to thieves. Newspaper and online articles regularly inform the public that the museum's copy "is held in a secure off-site location." However, it's shown once a year during the weekend-long festival in mid-July, which happened to be coming up this weekend, because the rider carrying the Dunlap Broadside finally made it into town on July 16, 1776.

The American Independence Museum hosts a big festival event on site as well as on the nearby Swasey Parkway along the Exeter River. It is complete with the ritual arrival and public reading of the Declaration by a John Taylor Gilman impersonator, costumed colonial characters, battle reenactors, cannon firings and a parade. Nearly four thousand people attend each summer, some from quite far away.

Just last week, Maryvonne had read a big article in the newspaper highlighting the new story-path and the annual showing of the broadside. It said that the Dunlap Broadside would be shown in a large glass case down the hill in the Folsom Tavern, a new display location for this year's American Independence Festival. Little did Maryvonne know then how she and her spangle would soon become entangled with Exeter's Dunlap.

Today was Thursday, and Maryvonne knew attendees and presenters would begin to trickle in later today - right near the very spot she was painting in this early morning. She was not a big fan of painting in crowds, but she was under a time crunch. Unfortunately, the airbag incident had set her back by more than a few days, so she had to focus today and get the painting done before the crowds came. Then she could bring it home and let it dry for a day, and then cover the whole painting in a thick coat of gloss and let that also dry before bringing it to the auction at the town hall.

But the slightly funny tingle and lingering shreds of headache in the faded purple bump on her forehead were a mismatch with the music. Dang. She reluctantly pulled the earbuds out by their purple string, deciding to put them back in later when people started milling about. The earphones could at least function as a decoy to dissuade people from talking to her, so she could focus on her work and get in the flow.

The flow was a place she loved to visit. But she had to get the mechanics of the set-up out of the way first.

Twisting the brass knobs tightly on her easel, she then gave it a little shake to ensure that the white canvas was solidly attached. She pulled on the tiny brass handle to open the small drawer that held her acrylic paints, brushes, knives, pencils, chalk, rags and plastic palette. She selected a 3H pencil. From out of her large purse, she took her purple plastic water sprayer and matching small plastic water jar with a wire loop at the top. She poured an inch of water into the jar, then hung it on a small hook her husband had affixed to the easel when he customized it for her.

This simple action caused her to think of her husband, who had gifted her with the customized French easel. The kids and grandkids all called him Zeus, and she still adored him as much as the day they were married eight years ago. He was an even-keeled Libra with a mass of silver curls, clear blue eyes, and the energy of a much younger man. During her airbag convalescence he had been a prince, keeping her ice packs cold, her ibuprofen on schedule and cooking her delicious food to boot. She smiled a most contented smile at the thought of him, let out a small sigh, and said "mon chéri."

Maryvonne was a blonde, green-eyed, tall and ample woman of French heritage with a big happy smile that lit up a room, and an easy laugh to match. She was bilingual, so French words would slip into her conversations and exclamations and that was part of her magic. In the parking lot of the market last week, she had seen the car coming and was in the middle of some very, very bad French words when the airbag deployed in her face and knocked the wind right out of her. If she was not still so angry about the annoyance of it all, she would have thought her foul French words quite funny.

But now she was very, very happy. The sun was shining, she loved summer, and she loved to paint. Maryvonne was known for painting all her skies yellow, and this time would be the same, so that at least was a given. But what shade of yellow would do to compliment this scene and convey the tone? Cadmium Yellow, Yellow Oxide, Bismuth Yellow, Yellow Ochre - hmm. So much fun pushing colors around! But she would get to that later. First she needed to decide on her composition.

Putting on her bi-focal glasses, she peered across the street to get a good look at the house from this angle. She looked at how the windows were set into the house in relation to the chimneys as she sized up the composition. She pondered this for just a minute and then raised the pencil to the canvas. The foreground would be just a bit of the branches and leaves of the small chokecherry tree dappling the sunshine close over her head. Mid-ground would be the tavern itself, and the background would be the old stone wall and a fuzzy bit of the yellow house on the small hill. She looked across the street to line up the branch with the tavern and began to sketch.

From around the far corner of the Folsom Tavern came Joe, the baker and owner of Joe Saints; he was holding an oversized reusable shopping bag emblazoned with the logo of the supermarket she had shopped at just before the accident. "Mon Dieu" she thought to herself and rolled her eyes. Which caused a bit of a spangle in her head and took a good few seconds to whirl away.

The bag was very full of large baguettes, peeking higgledy-piggledy out the top and popping up and down madly as Joe quickly crossed the street and went hurriedly in between his shop and the building on the far side of it, towards the shop's back entrance. Maryvonne was seated in the shadow of the tree and Joe seemed to not see her from that distance - and she was glad, because he was a chatterer.

In between batches of baked goods slipping in and out of his large ovens, Joe would come out to the front with a dusting of flour in his curly red hair and sit with the regular customers for a quick minute and chat about sports, town politics or his favorite subject: birding. Maryvonne was a member of one of the local klatches that called his shop home, so was very well known to him.

Usually she was up for a chat to defend the feminist view or comment on the doings around town, but not today, so she was glad he did not appear to have seen her. In the quiet morning light, her creative process was just starting to bubble. The kaleidoscope of prospective angles of the painting was beginning to take shape in her mind. She began to move her hand across the canvas, lightly penciling in the shapes and shadows. Dappled leaves in the foreground, angled corner of the house with prominent granite steps in the mid, curving story-path and lilac bushes and suggestion of the upper treasury house rising above an old stone wall in background. That would do nicely. "Bon," she said aloud, pleased with her progress.

While blocking in the sketch, she had to keep taking her bifocals off and putting them back on. But still, she could not quite make out what that dark, round thing was beyond the path and atop the stone wall. Too far away. Resigning herself to getting up and walking over there to inspect the thing, she arose from her small portable chair, stretched her arms overhead, flicked a wayward slip of bang away from her eye, then went to the curb and waited.

A single car passed and then she crossed over to the far sidewalk. She stepped onto the grass, glanced back at her easel, then headed toward the stone wall. She got just past the lovely story-path, stopped and looked up at the thing atop the old wall: it was a modern-day plastic compost barrel with a hand-crank. Maryvonne was always interested in green and sustainable living, but she was unsure whether to keep the bin in the painting, or eliminate it.

Pondering this dilemma, she turned to go but noticed something at her feet. A piece of the grass had been cut in a two-foot square of sod, but was barely noticeable. The cut was perfect and the ground was still very flat and undisturbed. Maryvonne stopped and wondered what it could be. Then she remembered that she had read in the newspapers that archaeologists had been hired to dig test pits near the two buildings before the museum could lay a conduit between them. This must be one of the test pits.

The article said they would dig ten random test pits, four feet deep, taking almost a week to do so. And this was just last week, so the deed was done and things were all flattened out in time for the festival. Maryvonne stared at the square and briefly wondered how anyone could be so precise in the slicing and digging and returning of the sod, and more importantly had they found any artifacts of interest? She turned away from the barely noticeable cut and headed back to her lonely easel by the cement column across the street in the dappled morning shade.

But now she stopped on the new looping story-path to admire the remnants of a spectacular pink peony bush near a placard. The path was a stunning landscape design of curves and flowering bushes of varying heights that afforded walkers small eddies of intimacy with tiny whimsical wrought iron benches on which to sit as they read the informational placards.

This was her very first time on the new path. Planners and designers had used it to connect the two masculine-dominated houses with a thread of Revolutionary era female history via a young cousin of Nicholas and John Taylor Gilman, "Tabitha (Gilman) Tenney (1762-1837)," and her young bi-racial friend "Rhoda Paul (1769 -1844)" who would later marry the famous African-American New Hampshire patriot "Jude Hall (1760-1827)." Maryvonne paused to read the plaques telling this story, which she found very compelling.

As she looked at the etchings of their faces, she could have sworn the sketch of Tabitha moved ever so slightly. Maryvonne shook her head, blinked, and looked again. Nothing moved and that was good. Calmed, she began to read again.

She was astonished to learn of the extent of the Black community that lived in Exeter just after the Revolutionary war; at 4.6 percent it was the largest in the entire state. This was news to her. How could she have missed that fact? Why wasn't this distinction better known? How could such a large chunk of important history be missing? She had never seen any physical manifestation of this distinction around town in the usual form of a statue, bench, park, building or street name. The way the town presented now, it seemed like Black folks had never thrived there.

But filling in this missing bit of history was precisely the point of the story-path, and the designers had done a good job.

Knowing she should get back to her easel, which she glanced at every so often, she decided to spend a few more minutes on the story-path. Trying out one of the ornate iron seats, she settled in and read the next placard about Tabitha, Rhoda and Jude. Tabitha Gilman was born and lived in Exeter during the American Revolution; she was fourteen when independence from England was declared. The Gilman family had been in town for nearly one hundred years by the time she was born, and the family had blossomed into a large presence of town fathers: mill owners, bankers, preachers, and more.

But the surviving records are all about the Gilman men. Very few Gilman women have left a mark on the town's history. Tabitha was to grow to be one of them, and indeed leave her mark on the entire country.

According to the placard, Tabitha spoke very slowly, deliberately choosing words, but her mind was very fast and sharp. She could be compared to Thomas Jefferson's daughter Martha in regard to her intense amount of self-education, alas, basically in vain. Too much education for a girl at that time actually, so she had to dumb herself down to avoid leaving a wake of sadly shaking heads everywhere she went. Tabitha's formative years were spent in the background, listening to her male relatives as they planned New Hampshire's contribution to the Revolution, and the making of a new independent country called America. She took it in like a sponge, and formed her own theories, but remained silent. As respectable women did in those days.

But Tabitha would become one of early America's very first female novelists, publishing (anonymously at first) a somewhat feminist story in 1801 that was also sympathetic to Blacks. Her satirical novel *Female Quixotism* would become a fifty-year bestseller, go through five printings, and be studied later by feminist scholars in the era of Women's Lib and beyond. At twenty-six years old, about ten years later than most girls of the era, Tabitha would finally marry a local doctor. She would never have children.

Maryvonne found the displays most compelling and she spent a bit of time reading them, lost in thought. Crinkling her brow, she wondered why she only thought of men when it came to the Revolutionary time period, just now having an epiphany that there had always been something missing: not many stories of women or Blacks or other non-whites were recorded or shared, aside from the classic tropes.

The board at the Revolutionary non-profit had decided it was time to share an honest and inclusive truth, so they had made this story-path. Softening her gaze, Maryvonne felt glad that they did. A certain part of her head and heart connected and became whole, like joining two puzzle pieces, which made her smile inside her eyes. Suddenly she heard a rustling noise close by which startled her from her ruminations. Out of the corner of her eye something flickered. She saw someone in the backyard of the tavern, cutting through, close by the lilac bushes at the house.

It was Brent Wickingham III, a teacher from the prep school next door, heading to Joe Saints for morning coffee. Brent crossed the street and went to the door and entered, becoming Joe's first customer of the day. Maryvonne had often seen him in the coffeeshop while she was in there chatting with her friends. She heard both teachers and students saying hello to him, so she knew his name and that he was a new history department teacher. She finished reading the placard, stood up, smoothed her pants, and quickly returned to her easel across the street. Time was ticking away.

She finished off her pencil sketch in a jiffy. Now it was time to add the color - her favorite part. Opening the tiny drawer on her easel, she slid it towards her and pulled out her plastic pallet and then selected three brushes. Around her waist she tied her art apron and inserted the brushes in the big front pocket.

Next, she started looking at the colors... which yellow would she choose for the sky? She was thinking now in an inclusive feminine vein, since reading about Tabitha Gilman and her friends. Contemplating how she could possibly convey some feeling of femininity into her painting of the Tavern, it settled over her that she would paint it in a very sunny and slightly washed out yellow tone with bright splashes of magenta in the flora. Yes, that would lighten the starkness from what the somber dark-brown and mustard scene actually presented.

Settled on her choice of artistic feeling she began selecting tubes of paints for this painting. In her whimsical mind, Maryvonne often thought of each tube as a friend. Yellow was always the first friend in the line-up, and often she painted the entire canvas in a yellow-wash undercoat as a first step. She chose a buttery Bismuth Yellow and slipped it in her apron pocket. Lots of white would be very important to keep the scene full of light, so that tube joined yellow in her pocket. Magenta, Cerulean Blue, Sap Green. These five friends would make up the palette.

Out of the drawer now came a kneaded art-eraser mashed into a streaky grey ball, which she rubbed lightly over the pencil lines to remove any possibility of pencil smudge. Lightly brushing off any debris, she was ready for the yellow undercoat.

A hearty squeeze of the yellow tube sent a long streak of thick paint snaking onto her plastic palette. Two long sprays of water from the sprayer melted over the soft yellow snake, and with a large brush Maryvonne began mixing it into a runny dilution in one corner of the palette. Brush full of yellow, she began painting long strokes across the sketch, covering the entire canvas with a yellow wash, which sealed in the light pencil sketch, still visible under the thin coating. Maryvonne leaned back against one of the square cement poles holding up the mod overhang of the office building, inspected the job, and decided it was a good coverage. Plopping the yellow brush into the hanging water jar for a quick cleaning and drying with a rag, she let the canvas air-dry while she went to buy a cup of coffee inside the shop.

Joe Saints was now open for business, and the first few early-birds were coming and going, letting the old wooden screen door slap behind them. She entered and let the door slap too. It was a sound from her youth, before everyone had pneumatic arms to silently swish their doors shut. Maryvonne chose a dark French Roast, which surged black and steamy into her portable mug, she screwed on the lid, paid the cheery Brenda Sue who presided above the pastries in the glass display counter, and was back outside in a flash.

Seated in front of her drying canvas under the chokecherry tree, she removed the lid and blew on the hot cup of coffee while looking around at the way the sun was now casting shadows on the tavern. After a few more cooling puffs, it was time: Maryvonne took a sip of that hot coffee and it tasted like heaven. Ahhh. She smiled. Joe Saints had the best coffee in town and the wave of coffee bean goodness rose into her head, soothing like a warm bath, and took the edge off her receding headache. She drank almost half of it, then decided to sip on the rest as the balmy morning grew contentedly into a warm afternoon. The cuppa joe was good, life was good, and the headache was soothed away into something different, like a small vibration that let the edges of her mind loosen and overhang.

Setting the mug down on the square cement planter near her small seat, she inserted the decoy earbuds. Carefully testing the yellow wash on the canvas with one finger to find it was dry enough, she began squeezing all the chosen colors into a ring of acrylic blobs on her palette. Spray-water spritzed the colorful ring with one quick spurt, only to keep the dryness away. The Filbert brush was her go-to; she took a deep breath and hunkered down with it in hand and began swishing the first colors onto the canvas. Daubing and blending... Layering and complementing... Looking up at the scene - looking straight at the canvas - looking down at the palette. And again. Blending, layering, looking up then down. Around and around she went in her mind until she spiraled into the aloneness and oneness of connection with her art flow. Maryvonne was firmly in that flowing space many people never reach. The hours drifted by.

Inside her misty, art-flowing mind, Maryvonne smelled roses and looked up to see a young lady on the far sidewalk carrying a large antique flower-gathering basket filled with gorgeous flowers: a bundle of heirloom red roses, another of feathery white yarrow, and a third bundle of delicate blue cornflowers. Each bundle was tied separately with long white ribbons. The girl's light brown hair was piled on her head in an intricate bun from which loose curls dangled over her pale forehead in the soft breeze. She wore a long flowing dress of yellow cotton in the Empire style, accented with soft blue ribbons. Maryvonne was caught off guard to see this vision of loveliness coming towards her, and thought the girl must be an actress already in character for the festival. She put her paint brush in the hanging water jar, pausing to look up again at the girl and her attractive red, white, and blue flowers. It was quite a patriotic sight of youth and beauty.

From behind the billowing yellow skirt Maryvonne was surprised to see another girl appear, dressed in the same style, but this one was much younger with dark hair and tan skin, and carrying a single red rose in her hand. The youngster ran to catch up, returning the dropped rose to the basket. Then the two girls held hands and passed right by Maryvonne, the older one giving her a slight nod. She turned her head around to see where they were going.

As Maryvonne turned, she was stunned to see a teen-aged boy at the entrance to the building behind her. He was strongly built and about seventeen years old, with beautiful deep black skin and expressive eyebrows. His foot was heavily bandaged, and he was sweeping the planks of the wooden entrance with a very old-fashioned twig broom. He looked up and smiled just as the two girls stopped in front of him. "Good day Miss Tabby. Doctor Tilton just stepped out to post a letter to his partner, Doctor Tenney, who is tending to the fighters down Boston way, but he will be right back," he said merrily. At the mention of the young Doctor Tenney's name Tabby's eyes seemed to sparkle and her smile grew.

The handsome and loquacious young man went on, "I see you have some yarrow for us today, and we sure do appreciate that, and look at those roses! Your family gardens are some of the best in town Miss Tabby."

She smiled again and replied, speaking clearly and slowly as if she were royalty, "Why good morning to you Scipio. It is nice to see you. How is your foot today?" Maryvonne was quite surprised by the girl's speech and bearing, since Maryvonne took her to be only about fourteen or fifteen years old.

"Coming along just fine," replied the boy. "Doctor Tilton says I'll be able to take off the bandages by next month. I'll always limp, but at least he didn't have to amputate my whole foot and I'm thankful to the Almighty

Lord for that." Then he leaned down and tickled the little girl under the chin and said to her, "I'll be happy to put on two shoes again. They won't be quite as pretty as your little slippers, Miss Rhoda, but I'm going to do a little dance on that day, and you can come watch me do it." Then he wiggled around with his broom just a bit which made the little girl giggle.

"I'll sing you a song to dance to on that day!" she declared and a lovely and low sing-song voice flowed like a river from her small lips, "Scipio will dance a jig, with his broom made of twig..." And now, Maryvonne was really surprised by the dulcet voice that came out of this little girl. It seemed very mature and melodious for a girl all of maybe seven years old.

"Oh, my little songbird," sighed Scipio, clutching at his heart, "I am going to marry you when you grow up, just to hear you sing every day." Little Rhoda blushed and giggled some more.

Tabby set down the basket of flowers near the door, put her hands on her hips and cleared her throat and with her chin high said, "Miss Rhoda has been doing very well in her singing and elocution lessons under my tutelage this past year. Her grandfather, attorney Rollins, is encouraging this and paying her tuition. Currently, Rhoda is staying at my house for special lessons while her mother Mrs. Lovey goes with attorney Rollins to Boston for a week-long visit."

She went on to explain, "Mrs. Lovey plans to shop for fine fabrics while grandfather Rollins attends some important meeting with other lawyers. Now Scipio, I fear I cannot have Miss Rhoda become betrothed while they are away. It just would not do!" She arched an eyebrow and waggled a finger at him, all the while with a hint of a smile at the corners of her lips.

"You are quite right Miss Tabby, and anyway my little brother Jude told me on the day he ran away to join the militia last year that he was going to come back a free man and marry little Miss Rhoda, so I should keep her safe until he returns." At this, little Rhoda's big brown eyes flew open, her tan cheeks turned a deep shade of crimson, and she looked silently at the ground.

"Oh, you and your clever talk, Scipio," began Tabby slowly, "look at her - you have indeed put a charm on the poor girl. It is a rare moment that she is quiet as a mouse."

Then leaning over and scooping up the bundle of yarrow from the basket she handed it to him. "Please give these to Doctor Tilton for his apothecary. They are such robust specimens - and I was already on my way to my cousin Nicholas's house across the street with these roses and cornflowers to make an arrangement in his receiving room - I thought it a shame to keep all this yarrow in my gardens when they could be put to good medicinal use."

"Miss Tabby, you have such a fine head on your shoulders, you think differently than other girls in town," Scipio said becoming serious as he weighed the feathery yarrow in his hand. "For a minute I thought these were the wild carrot we had discussed last week in regards to your question on certain ladies' complaints," and he gave a little chuckle. "These yarrow are very robust indeed. Since my accident last year, I have been working with the herbs in Doctor Tilton's apothecary and have come to know the weak from the powerful stems and blossoms." Then he stopped and a wave of melancholy flickered across his expressive eyebrows.

"You know Miss Tabby, God works in mysterious ways. Jude and I had both heard the news that any slave from New Hampshire that fought against the British would become free after three years of service. We decided we would both run away from farmer Blake the very next week and join up. But then I had my accident before I could leave.

And Jude, well you know Jude made it. I am sure proud of the news from the fighting at Bunker Hill last month. He could always fight, my little brother, yes ma' am. I could never get the best of him; it was quite vexing." At that memory he brightened and continued, "And like I said, God works in mysterious ways: because of the accident farmer Blake couldn't use me to work in the fields anymore so he sold me to the Doctor, and I am about as happy as I can be, given the circumstances."

At that Tabby pursed her lips, lowered her chin and stared right into Scipio's eyes and said slowly, "If it were up to me, there would be none of this enslavement nonsense. A man is a man, and all should be free to do as he pleases and earn his own keep." Scipio held her gaze with sad eyes. Little Rhoda stared at the ground again. This quiet trio was interrupted by a commotion from across the street.

Running down from the yellow house up on the hill came a slim young man in a fancy green waistcoat and brown breeches, holding his brown tri-cornered hat steadily on his head as he bounced towards them. He was a round-faced boy who appeared a couple of years older than Scipio but did not, and would never, have the muscular girth of the former farm slave.

Tabby turned at the sound of his running footsteps. "Why John Taylor Gilman, whatever has gotten into you?" she inquired, in her slow manner of speech.

"Cousin Tabby, I thought that was you I saw out the window. Listen now, very important. Indeed," he huffed, out of breath from the run, but the words flowed on out of his small mouth. "Indeed. A rider delivered a message from Philadelphia to the house just now. There is to be a public reading of the message in two hours' time on the steps of the Town House on Front Street. Indeed. Nicholas has asked me to read it, and to get the Reverend to give a blessing before the reading, which I shall do next.

But betwixt we also need a song to commemorate that which is just now being born. A young voice is what we need. A psalm. To manifest a spirit of devotion to the cause of liberty. Indeed. Tabby, I need you to practice your little songbird pupil in the next two hours to be ready to sing Billings' psalm *America* from the steps before the reading."

Tabby nodded and John Taylor turned to Scipio and gasped out his final sentence, "Both of you, tell everyone you see to be at the steps in two hours' time, please." And leaving as quickly as he had come, John Taylor ran off towards the Congregational Church in search of Reverend Rumpole, still holding his jiggling hat upon his round head.

"What do you think the message is?" asked little Rhoda, her eyes wide. Tabby and Scipio looked at each other with concern and said at the same time, "War."

"I must take my leave, Scipio, I do apologize for the haste, but I must quickly arrange these flowers in a vase of water for Nicholas then go rehearse my pupil," Tabby said, as she picked up the basket of red and blue flower bundles and took Rhoda's small hand. Scipio and Rhoda said their goodbyes, and Scipio turned, moving as quickly as he could on his incomplete foot and took the yarrow bundle into the shop, the old wooden door slapping behind him.

The girls crossed the street hand-in-hand, the white ribbons from the flower bouquets streaming out behind them as they quickly walked, feet kicking up small clouds of dust. The pair were singing the requested psalm in unison, which also flowed out behind them as they rose up the hill, fading into the yellow house:

"Come, let us sing unto the Lord,
And praise His name with one accord.
In this design one chorus raise,

From east to west His praise proclaim,
From pole to pole extol His fame,
The skies shall echo back His praise."

Maryvonne stood gaping, almost dizzy with confusion. She squeezed her eyes shut, shook her head rapidly and took a sharp inward breath. She felt the overhang in her mind spangle and quiveringly slip back into the confines. When she opened her eyes again, she almost fell over into her easel. Blinking and slowly exhaling, she looked around astonished at the scene of this century: the glass doors, cement posts and paved roads.

Chapter 2

Will the wind remember the names it has blown in the past?
And the wind cries Mary

Thinking she was about to have some kind of fit, she had quickly packed up her easel and driven directly home. Zeus was in the kitchen just pulling a tray of blueberry muffins out of the oven. The muffins smelled wonderful and Maryvonne suddenly realized she had skipped breakfast, and had only been running on coffee for the past three hours or so. Her doctor would not have been pleased.

Standing in the kitchen wearing oven mitts and holding one of the muffin tins, Zeus said, "How did the painting go?" He set down the tin on the counter and reached back inside the oven. "I was not expecting you back for another hour, but you're just in time if you want a hot muffin." Closing the door, he set the second tin on a rack alongside the first one to cool and took off the mitts.

Maryvonne smiled weakly and he could tell something was not quite right. "I think I stayed out too long for my first time back," she said quietly. "I would love a muffin, thank you, then I am going to lie down for a while. Could you please get my easel out of the car later when you get a chance?"

Zeus sat her down at the kitchen island and brought her a glass of water, which she drank while he pried two steaming muffins out of the tin and put them on small plates. He brought them over, then sat beside her. The muffins smelled heavenly and suddenly Maryvonne realized she was quite famished. Zeus cut open the muffins and smoothed on some fresh butter, which melted immediately. Sliding the enticing plate towards her, he said, "Be careful, my love, they are very, very hot."

While waiting for them to cool, Zeus informed Maryvonne that her car had been returned from the shop as good as new, and that he had parked it in the garage for her. That news made her happy. Then Maryvonne told him very briefly of her morning painting, omitting the last part where she had hallucinated.

Finally biting into the muffin, she savored it and then said, "Delicious, mon chéri, you have perfected your recipe." She continued, "The painting is ninety-five percent done, but I just had to come home and rest. The show is being hung early Saturday afternoon for the Sunday auction, so I have until one o'clock Saturday to bring the painting in. It should all work out fine." She continued eating the delicious muffin then said more to herself than Zeus, "I will give it a full gloss tomorrow before I put on the finishing touches.

Eating the last crumbs of the muffins she turned directly to her husband. "Thank you for the muffin, mon chéri, it was just what I needed. I am going up to bed now for a while."

Alone in the darkened bedroom, she finally allowed herself to set her mind to thinking about her hallucination and what it could mean.

Did the airbag really damage her mind? It had to be related as nothing like this had ever happened to her before. Was this some sort of mental disorder? Was she suddenly clairvoyant or able to "channel"? Was she simply dehydrated and overtired? Realizing that she did have a very active and creative imagination, she decided it was kind of fun to think that she had witnessed a shadow of the past.

With this thought she drifted off to a very deep and refreshing sleep.

Chapter 3

Can you see me?
Can you hear me crying all over town?

Three hours later Maryvonne woke up and checked the clock. *Mon Dieu!* she said to herself. How could she have slept for three hours? She really must have been tired. And now she was really hungry too. After freshening up in the bathroom, she went downstairs in search of food. On the counter was a note from Zeus saying that he was out playing tennis with his usual group and that he had left a bowl of tuna salad in the fridge for her. Maryvonne opened the door to the fridge and looked in. Tuna, pickles, milk all came out. After pouring a glass of milk, she set to work making two sandwiches on the cutting board by the sink. Lots of tuna, with pickles on top, on sourdough.

Taking a big knife, she sliced them both in half diagonally and picked up one of the halves and moved over the sink to eat it and think. This she thought of as a sinkee-sandwich. A mystery series author she had read decades ago used the term copiously and Maryvonne had used it ever since. At the first bite, she thought of the mystery author and his adventures in Florida and how he would not have much work in Exeter, as it was such a benign town.

Maybe it would be fun to have a crime or two to shake the place up? Like perhaps the swindling of residents who thought they were helping to restore the historic yet dilapidated Ioka movie theater? Or the heist of the town's precious Dunlap? Or the kidnapping and ransom of a town official? She laughed at the absurdity and took a second bite of the sinkee.

The advantage of the sinkee was little mess to clean up after, a nice view out the window of the forsythia bush, and time to think on her feet. Munching on her first half, she brushed away her frivolous thoughts and started thinking about Tabby, Rhoda and Scipio. What to make of it? She chewed and she thought some more. The dog smelled the tuna and came nosing by. She scratched the fluffy golden hair on his head and broke off an edge of her sandwich for him. He happily took it and ran off to chew it in the corner.

By the time she had finished all parts of both sandwiches and the milk, she knew where she was going next. She was going to see the Brim. The Brim would know. The Brim worked at the Historical Society and knew all, which was why the townsfolk affectionately referred to her as "the Brim": full to the brim with knowledge. Plus, no one could pronounce her real last name. Her first name began with B, and her last name started with Rim, then went on like a freight train from a foreign land. So, the Brim it became.

The Historical Society had limited hours, and one of the times they were open was Thursdays from two to four-thirty. The kitchen clock said half-past two. Good, that gave her time to apply the first thick coat of gloss to her painting, then drive over for a quick visit.

In her cellar she had a small art studio space, and thankfully Zeus had lugged her stuff down there before taking off with his Miata. Maryvonne's quick exit this morning from under the tree had left her French easel and art bag in disarray. She took some time to straighten everything out then set the canvas down flat on the work table. Shaking up a bottle of Liquitex Gloss Medium & Varnish until it was well blended, she flipped open the cap and squeezed about a tablespoon of the gooey liquid in each quadrant. With a damp sponge brush she brushed the gloss into one continuous smooth sheet from bottom to top, then diagonally to make sure there were no missing spots. Then she smoothed out the small dribbles that had dripped over the edges and on to the table. The final strokes went from side to side. Looking at it from all angles, she decided it was a good, even job and went upstairs to clean all her brushes from this morning with soapy water in the sink.

Pressing brushes this way and that into the soapy water at the sink, Maryvonne realized that this was the best she had felt in days. The fresh air, the nap and the food had revved up her energy level, and she was feeling quite back to normal. Even her headache was gone for the moment. Delighted about her return to health, she wrote out a quick note to Zeus and headed out in her fresh-from-the-repair-shop Ford electric hybrid to see the Brim.

The yellow brick sandstone building was a handsome classical structure that once housed the town public library, until it was outgrown. She slid the silent Ford into an empty parking spot right out front. Up the steps, under the arch and through the large wooden door and she was in the cool and quiet interior. Inside, it smelled like olde things, like grandparents' attics and antique bookshops, and Maryvonne loved it. Off to the right was the Brim, seated at a table with piles of papers and folders spread before her. The Brim peered up through her glasses and greeted Maryvonne. They attended the same church and knew each other well. Maryvonne loved her dry wit. After exchanging a few small pleasantries, Maryvonne got to the point of her visit.

"Are you familiar with Tabitha Gilman Tenney and Rhoda Hall?" asked Maryvonne.

"Oh yes, I have written many articles on Tabitha, and on Rhoda's husband Jude Hall in the past," answered the Brim, her mind clicking into historian mode. "And recently the American Independence Museum people were here researching for their new story-path project. I'm very pleased with how the path came out, have you seen it yet?"

"Yes, I just saw it this morning and I totally love the female angle," Maryvonne replied. At this they each raised one finger to their face and gave each other the fem-eye, for they were both awake to feminist issues.

"Now Tabitha is an easier one than Rhoda, since she is a Gilman. There are many Gilman primary sources.

But Rhoda is much trickier. Let me start with Tabitha." The Brim then related the story of Tabitha at length.

In a nutshell, it was as follows:

Tabitha was born to Samuel and Lydia Gilman. Samuel was born in the Gilman-Garrison House, one of the oldest homes in Exeter, but it's unknown where Tabitha was born and lived as a child with her siblings. Not much is known of her childhood. However, her adult home is well known. It stood alongside the Congregational Church but was later relocated and now stands at 65 High St, and has a historical marker on it bearing her name. She came of age at the time of the declaration of independence from England in the mid 1770's. Her family had been influential in town for a hundred years already. Some, like her uncle Brigadier Peter Gilman, were Tories loyal to the crown during the Revolution. Others, like her uncle Major John Gilman, were patriots and also had fought in the French and Indian Wars. Major John fought with his slave, Caesar Paul, at his side - until Caesar was captured by the French and taken as a prisoner of war.

Tabitha did not marry until she was twenty-six and this was highly unusual. And she never had any children, which was also unusual. Perhaps she knew things. (At this The Brim gave the fem-eye again.) Tabitha's husband, Dr. Samuel Tenney, was a physician, then a Congressman in Washington, then a judge in Exeter. And he was also a player. There is a paper trail of his dual romancing. Still remaining are his flirty notes sealed with wax, as well as the diary of the "other woman" during their courtship, Patty Rogers. Patty pines away for him, and other men including a preacher, and finds Tabitha quite unpleasant. Patty never marries, even after all that overly-dramatic pining that flows from her quill. Tabitha marries Dr.

Tenney, twenty years her senior, and they moved to Washington for a few years before returning permanently to Exeter to live in the new house they had built next door to the church. It's in this house in an upstairs room that she is rumored to have written her famous book.

When she published this book, *Female Quixotism, Exhibited in the Romantic Opinions and Extravagant Adventures of Dorcasina Sheldon,* she was not listed as the author. It is perhaps by the time the third (of five) printing came out that her name was finally attributed. The book was a smash hit, and still is readable and funny today. Having her name attributed to it caused shame in the town, because stepping out of the kitchen shadows like that was very unwomanly. Very much so. A later newspaper account from the 1920's Exeter Newsletter entitled "About Tabitha Gilman Tenney" continues to showcase this lingering sentiment. It talks mostly about her husband, male cousins, uncles... and then finally, sadly remembers her as a "Blue Stocking." This was a derogatory phrase meaning a member of the Blue Stocking Society, a Georgian era movement to encourage women towards intellectual and literary pursuits. Tut-tut. (Fem-eye again.)

Of her, no portrait, diary, or letters remain. Although she did write three books, only the smash hit still exists. It was reprinted most recently in 1991 by Oxford University Press with a forward by feminist scholars. Not too shabby, Tabby! Locally, two anecdotes survive. The first is that when she heard the news of the death of George Washington, she calmly put down the mirror she was holding, and then smoothed her skirts out before fainting. (Or feinting

> perhaps.) The other anecdote is a saying that lived on in Exeter for a hundred years: "You speak as slowly as Tabby Tenney." She outlived her husband by decades, and the two of them are buried under matching white stones in the historic Winter Street Cemetery.

"I say we form an Exeter chapter of the Blue Stocking Society in her honor," chortled Maryvonne. "*The Exeter Indomitables* sounds like a good name. We both already know a bunch of women and femmes around town who fit that description."

"I'm in," the Brim laughed and reached down to pull up the hem of her pants and show off her blue paisley socks, "and I already have the socks!" She let the hem drop and continued, "Now about Rhoda Hall, the story is not so happy." She then relayed this information to her sister Blue Stocking:

> Rhoda Paul was born free to former slave Caesar Paul and his white wife Lovey Rollins. Lovey was one of the children of white lawyer Caleb Rollins of Stratham. They lived out on Guinea Road on the Stratham line. Caesar originally lived at Major John Gilman's home on Cass Street as an enslaved house and body servant. He was described as a small and dark man. The two men went to the French and Indian Wars together and Caesar was captured and brought to Canada for a number of years. Major John had given up hope of regaining him so petitioned the government to reimburse him for the loss of his "property" and he received recompense. Years later, Caesar made it back to town. The story is unclear as to exactly why, but it seems that Caesar lived the rest of his life as a free man in Exeter as of 1771.

Caesar married Lovey and they had many children, one of them was Rhoda. Three of her brothers were schooled to become Baptist preachers. One brother, Reverend Thomas Paul, was extremely eloquent and captivating and became like a Martin Luther King of his time. He helped found the first Black Baptist church in Massachusetts and became its first pastor. This famous church is on the Black Heritage Trail in Boston at its headquarter complex on Beacon Hill. Rhoda's younger sister Nancy married a former slave who had made it to Exeter after running away from his enslavement in Virginia, and one of their children, born in Exeter on Elliot Street (originally Whitfield's Lane), became the abolitionist poet James Monroe Whitfield, a peer of Frederick Douglass, who went on to publish a book "America and other poems" in 1853.

Little is known of Rhoda herself, virtually nothing having been written or saved. She is a one-hundred-piece puzzle with only five pieces still in the box. What is known is that she married Revolutionary War veteran Jude Hall, a large and strong man formerly held in enslavement just over the Exeter line at a farm in Kensington, by Philemon Blake. The farm is on the same side of town that Rhoda's family lived on, both near the upper end of High Street.

After Jude returned from eight years in the war he had "earned" his freedom as well as a pension. They married and built a small two-room house quite near Blake's farm on Drinkwater Road. "Jude's Pond" is still on the town maps, and denotes their old homestead. Jude was well respected about town, and folks then referred to him as "Captain" or "Old

> Rock." Jude was profiled in several books written just after the war.
>
> Rhoda and Jude had ten or twelve children. Records are not too clear. But what is clear is that three of their grown sons were stolen and sold into slavery in the South: two sons were abducted when they were employed aboard ships out of Boston...

"But the third, the third son is where the story comes home to sit like a cactus in the heart of Exeter," said the Brim as she began glowering. Maryvonne leaned in with anxiety visible in her furrowed eyebrows as the story went on. She had read parts of it, but not all, in recent news articles.

> A Boston affidavit states: Jude was out of town when an Exeter resident burst into Rhoda's house on Drinkwater. Only Rhoda, her eighteen-year-old son James, and his younger sister Dorothy were home. The man was David Wedgewood and he claimed that James owed him four dollars, so he had the right to take him. Rhoda said he was a minor and for Wedgewood to leave him alone. A scuffle ensued and Wedgewood got the boy, bound him and immediately transported him to Newburyport where he was shipped out on a boat the next day, presumably bound for New Orleans.
>
> But then, confusingly, there is a conflicting report from a letter Rhoda sent to the Liberator newspaper in 1843. As well as a retort from Captain Isaac Stone of Newburyport.
>
> Then, there are recently discovered ship manifests from March 1819 that show James and three others as

the "property" of Hector McLean of New Orleans being shipped on the brig Ship Superb to McClean, from David Anderson of Baltimore.

Years later a report came back to Exeter that a local person had seen him in a jail in New Orleans. James had run away but was caught and was being held until his "owner" came. No other word ever came.

The whole affair is a foul mystery, yet unsolved.

Jude spent the rest of his life running from lawyer to judge, all to no avail. Today there is little paper trail, it would seem this tragic story was never printed or spoken about in town. Jude died in 1827 without ever seeing his three sons again. This American patriot was not treated well, and doubly so since his story was all but forgotten.

And his wife Rhoda, poor Rhoda, left town after Jude's death and moved to Belfast, Maine, to live with two of her married daughters until her death in 1844. The last half of her life must have been heavy with sadness. She and her daughters are buried in the Grove Cemetery in Belfast.

A stunned Maryvonne sat rapt. This sad story had been alluded to on the story-path, but the Brim knew it in all its heinous details. Maryvonne was shocked, then furious, then sad.

These emotions swirled around in her head so fast that she began to feel the strange overhang and spangle again. "Mon Dieu," she whispered, realizing that she lived within walking distance of this kidnapping site. Realizing that she walked in the footsteps of Jude, and Rhoda and James when she walked into town from her house on upper High Street. Realizing that if circumstances were different, it could be her sturdy little grandson that some hate-filled man in town was sizing up as a commodity while watching him grow big and strong until the day he decided to cash him in, or something along those lines. It was sickening. And it appeared the town did nothing.

Maryvonne's heart was breaking for Rhoda; her son literally ripped from her arms. It was all so crazy and unbelievable that it happened in this quiet little Northern town. She was speechless.

"Any other questions?" said the glowering Brim in a very tight and clipped voice.

Maryvonne answered in a distracted voice, "Is there anyone from this era by the name of Scipio?"

"Yes," she replied, caught a little off guard at the sudden tangent. "There may have been more than one Scipio. One Scipio was a well-liked slave in town who was very clever and came to all but run the business of his owner, who by all accounts was quite the slacker and very disliked. This is documented in a court case. Scipio changed his last name a few times so the records get fuzzy."

"Chapeau du cul"... "merde-morceau"... Maryvonne spoke these and other spur-of-the-moment French inventions under her breath as she drove up High Street towards home in a state of rage. What could she do about it? Nothing. How could she channel her rage to work for good? Impossible. She could think of nothing short of time-travel that would have any effect at all. She felt defeated already. It was ancient history.

Yes, she thought, that is exactly what it was: history. HIS-story. Probably ninety percent of all history is written by men, and tut-tut if a woman steps out of line: all she will get is bad press, if any. Tabby knew that all too well. Hmmpf. Perhaps Maryvonne could find a way to re-write it into a HER-story. Serendipitously, at that moment she suddenly remembered an ad she had recently seen in a college newsletter about something called a Wikipedia Edit-a-thon, sponsored by a group called Art + Feminism or something. It seemed like a good global outlet for a newly minted Exeter Indomitable. She would look into it and maybe spread some her-story around. To what effect she had no idea.

The Zeus-mobile was in the driveway when she pulled in. Walking into the kitchen she could hear television noises coming from the living room. Zeus was in his leather recliner with the dog beside him, watching the Red Sox at full blast, and drinking a can of lime soda water. She walked over to him and gave him a big hug and a kiss on the head.

"What is this all about?" he inquired.

"Oh, I am just so glad to see you, and so grateful that you are a kind and caring man. I just found out something awful, let me go get a glass of water and then I'll sit and tell you about it."

Sitting in the wing chair next to him while the ballgame played in the background at a low volume, she relayed the stories that the Brim had told her. He admitted that he had little knowledge of those parts of the town's history as well. In addition, she told him about her strange hallucination that morning. He looked concerned.

"Why didn't you tell me this morning?"

"I wasn't quite sure what to make of it, and I just wanted to take a nap."

"Next time please tell me. I would have stayed home from tennis to keep an eye on you."

"I know, and I didn't want that, mon chéri. I felt fine after a nap and big lunch. And I feel fine now." After a slight hesitation, she said what she was really feeling. "I don't think it was a hallucination. I think it was some kind of mystic vision or shadow of the past. Something is calling to me from the past for some reason. I don't know why...yet."

He looked at her in the way he did when she started talking about her unified-field theory, serendipity, and other ideas that were based on no sanctioned evidence, only intuition. She loved that "spooky action at a distance" spiritual stuff, loved the Feminine Divine and totally discarded the "rule by fear" of a patriarchal godhead. He, being a retired science teacher, believed only in the facts as presented by physics and chemistry.

"I tend towards leftover concussion, instead of mystic vision," he said rather flatly.

"I knew you would, but I still adore you," she said, giving him a big smile, and he laughed.

She went on, "I am going to go upstairs and check my email and change my shirt before I stop by the art opening tonight for a few minutes at Front & Center Studios at five o'clock. After that there is the book talk at seven. Did you still want to go to the Water Street Books & More with me then?"

"Depends how the game is going - it's a big game tonight. There could be a rain delay, but it should be over by then," he informed her as he turned up the volume again.

"I have heard that one before," she replied, rolling her eyes as she ascended the stairs, the words trailing behind her and getting lost in the roar of the cheering fans.

Chapter 4

You got a new fool, ha! I like it like that
Let me stand next to your fire

At five on the nose she parked on the crumbling sidewalks outside the Front & Center Gallery and Studios in the west end of town. This was Exeter's version of a converted art mill. The owner Elena Rose felt it very important to be both civic and creative. The motto of her gallery was painted on the front door and Maryvonne read it again as she passed over the threshold into the front gallery space: "Creativity and community are the essence of happiness and personal growth." Elena Rose also loved yellow and had recently painted over-sized yellow flowers on the outside of the grey building, and it looked fabulous to Maryvonne.

Usually the first thing Maryvonne did was to head straight through to the refreshment area to get a glass of red wine, and then bring it all the way back to the front gallery. Then she took great pleasure in viewing the art from the front gallery to the back gallery, sipping wine and chatting with other artists all the way. The final room was the pot of gold at the end of the journey. Elena Rose displayed her own pieces there: gorgeous paintings of organic forms, saturated with color. Maryvonne was a big fan of her sun-drenched style.

But tonight Maryvonne decided to forgo the wine, just in case it gave her a headache. Truth be told, a tiny bit of odd energy still lingered near the fringes now that the day had grown long. Maryvonne had entered the building and was standing in the crowd in the front gallery, so she stayed right there, said hello to a few of her friends from her weekly painting group, and began viewing the art.

This was Front & Center's annual summer show opening reception, to coincide with the American Independence Festival weekend. In an attempt to coordinate with the many offerings around town, the opening was held on a Thursday night instead of the usual Friday so as to work synergistically into the well publicized town-wide schedule. The theme of the show was

"Re.Evolution: Sustainability is Patriotic" and artists were showing all types of sustainable and earth-friendly art.

The front gallery, a bright white room, was awash in whimsical art on the patriotic theme of "American Flags." There were flags woven from various fibers including one of painted grasses, one from plastic apple-picking bags and another of (possibly) bra straps. There were flags painted on various-sized canvases, in various colors and shapes. There was one mosaic made from broken seashells and sea glass, and another made from plastic gleaned during a beach clean-up. It was a remarkable display of creativity. There was a close-up photo of a citizenship ceremony which featured a small man taking the Pledge with tears collecting on his moustache and a large flag behind him. Overall, Maryvonne thought, it was a terrific salute to the best of what it means to be a loving, happy, and generous American citizenry.

Maryvonne left the front gallery and began walking down the hallway of small studio spaces. Inside the first studio was a woman who crafted art quilts from odd scraps of industrial metals. She was working on a small quilt, reminiscent of the Betsy Ross thirteen colonies flags with a circle of stars. The exquisite piece was almost soft looking, somehow. This made Maryvonne think of Jude Hall again, as this must have been the style of flag that Jude fought under to gain his freedom. His and ours. She silently thanked Jude for his contributions to the founding of America.

Maryvonne went from studio to studio looking at paintings, pottery, wooden laser etchings and more - all the while greeting friends. Then she arrived at the back gallery and just basked in the glow of Elena Rose's sun-drenched paintings of flowers, trees, and birds. "Magnifique!" she said aloud to no one in particular as she stood in the center of the room. She closed her two eyes, focusing on her third, and for a brief second had the feeling that she was standing in the sunny and lush navel of the goddess Gaia. When she finally opened her eyes, they were smiling.

Her happy eyes were drawn to one painting in particular in which the leaves of the trees seemed to glow from behind. She went over and studied the work up close. The technique was very interesting and Maryvonne decided to take a picture of it on her cell phone and try it at home. Elena Rose's husband, Mal, had a desk in the side nook of the room, from which he ran a computer tune-up and repair business. She went over to the desk to set down her purse and get out her cell phone to take the picture. The phone had fallen to the bottom, and when she finally fished it out, her car keys came flying out as well. They landed on Mal's open laptop keyboard, and the machine blinked to life.

Maryvonne was embarrassed, and hoped she had done no damage. She went around behind the desk to inspect the computer to make sure nothing looked broken. The keyboard looked fine. Maryvonne's eyes scanned over the lit screen and she didn't see any scratches. But then her eyes caught on the words on the screen, and she stopped short. The document on the screen was entitled "Dunlap Broadside Heist Plan."

She felt a bit of a shock go through her system. Would Mal do something like that? Maryvonne glanced around the room and everyone was busy looking at the art, and not at her. She looked back at the screen. Under the title was a numbered list, and after each entry followed a dollar amount:

1. Obtain J. Green & Sons paper. VintagePaper.Com: $125
2. Print text on Konica bizhub at F&C gallery: $0
3. Obtain archival frame. MuseumFraming.com: $225
4. Hack security systems: $0
5. Switch out at night: $0

6. Sell for $8.1 million

8.1 million dollars? Maryvonne couldn't believe it. Big bucks! Was Mal seriously considering doing this? He had the computer skills, and the art gallery had tools that would be capable of producing a pretty convincing copy. Maryvonne was so taken aback by the thought that she slammed the laptop shut, threw her keys in her purse and headed for the front door. As she got closer, she saw there was a crowd in the front gallery now. A large group was clustered around someone in the center, and they were all laughing.

A voice rang out above the laughter. "Number four, hack security systems, zero, and number five, switch out at night, zero. So my total expenses are three hundred and seventy five. And then I will sell it for 8.1 million!" The crowd roared with laughter as Mal held aloft a printout of his list, which was attached to a stick so that it resembled a flag.

Maryvonne's artist friend Lucretia, who was in the laughing crowd, called out, "Is that is your patriotic retirement plan, Mal?"

"Yep, it sure is," he replied.

"Well, we know you probably do have the computer hacking skills," shouted out Skip, another of Maryvonne's artist friends. Mal gave him a high five.

Maryvonne saw her friend Susan in the crowd and went over to her. "What is going on here?" she asked hesitantly.

"Oh, it is just Mal being a clown. He is trying to convince Elena Rose this paper that he printed out should be hung in the patriotic flag exhibit. He tries to get in the art show every once in a while."

Maryvonne turned just in time to see Elena Rose kiss Mal on the forehead, turn him around, and shoo him out of the room saying, "Thanks, but no thanks, dear. You can try again at the next exhibition. That theme will be 'Pipelines of Wrath.' Good luck." Maryvonne laughed along with the crowd. But mostly at herself.

The Red Sox game was still playing on the television when she arrived home, and Zeus was in the kitchen cooking two pieces of salmon in a cast iron pan. He had the volume blasting, and kept peeking around the corner at the television. "How is the game going?" Maryvonne asked.

"Great game! Very exciting, it's been back and forth the whole time and it looks like it's going to go on for a while. It's a big game, if they can just win this one it's going to make all the difference," he said with his face all a-fan-glow. She could see at once that he would rather stay and watch the ending of the game than go to the bookstore to hear a lecture on the history of Early American footwear. Maryvonne was a bit of a shoe freak, so the talk did grab her imagination. The only reason that Zeus wanted to go was to see the author in action, who was a new history teacher at the same school where he had spent most of his career before retiring.

"Mon chéri, why don't you stay home and watch the game?" she said while picking up a knife and chopping Romaine lettuce he had set out on the cutting board. "I'm sure you will enjoy it more than the shoe lecture. I'll report back to you on what the young Mr. Brent Wickingham the third has to say." She got two salad bowls from the counter and divided the chopped lettuce evenly between them. Zeus laid the crispy salmon atop the lettuce, while Maryvonne got the salad dressing and brought it to the table. They ate the small meal quickly while listening to the game together.

Maryvonne arrived at Water Street Books & More about twenty minutes before the scheduled talk so she could browse the selection. This independent bookstore was a gem in town and the hub of Exeter's literary life, which was pretty impressive considering the size of the town. The store owners were a childless married couple, Stan and Effie, who finished each other's sentences. This habit caused them to be known affectionately around town as one entity called "Steffie."

Stan was a tall and thin Black man who was completely bald. He wore old-school black framed eyeglasses in the jazz style, and was a sharp dresser. He was into jazz and sometimes played the saxophone at gigs around town. He reminded Maryvonne of Miles Davis in some way. Effie was a short, Greek woman who got all the hair that Stan had lost. Her long, thick, dark curls hung to her waist in the fashion of a mermaid. She was a bit of a beat poet, and sometimes she would recite at Stan's gigs. Effie was also the driving force behind the town's annual spring literary festival called the Exeter LitFest.

The LitFest celebrated local poets and authors of all types, and Maryvonne was wondering if Brent would be profiled in next year's event with his '*Right Foot, Left Foot: Bipartisan Shoes for a Young America*', a small hardcover coffee-table book, when she saw him enter the shop. Brent was a sturdy young man with the pink look of the Scots about him. He wore his stick-straight strawberry blonde hair a bit long and slicked back in a euro-style, and had small green eyes. He greeted the owners and set down a large and heavy box of his books behind the podium.

"Jeez Brent, you didn't have to carry a whole case down here," Stan said. "We do carry it in inventory already, you know."

"No problem, I rolled it down with my collapsible trolley cart. I just left the cart outside while I do the talk. I plan on selling a ton of books, so I thought I would bring you some more inventory to replenish what we sell tonight. I just have one volunteer gig to wrap up this weekend, then I'm leaving town for the rest of the summer while school is out," Brent said in a slightly California surfer-dude accent.

While flipping pages to look at the pictures in a very large autobiography, Maryvonne overheard this exchange and was dubious about the number of books Brent would sell that night. She guessed twenty was the average for a local author at events like this. And given the topic, she was betting on ten at the max. The attendees began taking their seats in rows of folding chairs, and it seemed to Maryvonne that most of them were teachers from the history and sociology departments at the prep school. And then there were random women like her.

Some women really had some fun with shoes, and this self-selected group came to hear about shoes. As she often did when she was in a crowd, Maryvonne scanned everyone's footwear. She found that in addition to being one of her favorite forms of eye-candy, footwear always tells a story.

Yes, the women in the crowd did have on interesting shoes. She herself was wearing a pair of beautiful and soft leather mid-heel espadrille sandals from Spain in a shade of burnt honey, tied up around her ankles. She saw a lovely pair of navy Etienne Aigner sandals with gold horseshoe accents, a pair of hot-pink suede peep-toe kitten heels, a couple pair of white or silver Sperry boat shoes, and a young girl wearing comfy Havaianas flip-flops in soft-pink. The bookstore owner Stan was wearing camel-colored woven tassel-loafers with no socks, which befitted his coolness. Brent was wearing black Allbirds sneakers, high lace, in a faux Chuck Taylor style. Effie was standing behind the counter at the cash register, so

Maryvonne couldn't see her shoes, but she was usually wearing some kind of comfy European clog.

Stan turned on the podium microphone with a light feedback screech and tested the volume. He had a very large and powerful voice so it about blasted Maryvonne out of her seat causing her to look up from the feast of footwear. Stan adjusted the volume down and introduced himself, Effie, the bookstore, and the reason for this particular event tonight: as part of the American Independence Festival programming.

Then he began a quick introduction of Brent. Brent grew up in California, and went to college in England. He had been employed at the prep school for one year in the history department. Interestingly, Brent's family had been in footwear for a long time, and had actually invented spats. Spats! Of all things. Maryvonne knew little about spats except that they were small white cloths that buttoned over the top of shoes in the "olden" days to keep the mud and rain off. She remembered they were mentioned in the lyrics of the old tune "Puttin on the Ritz" and also that Gene Wilder had sung it in a macabre duet on screen in *Young Frankenstein* while both he and the dancing monster sported spats. It was hilarious and just thinking about it made her grin, and a little tune began playing in her head. *"White spats and lots of dollars, spending every dime, for a wonderful time. If you're blue and you don't know where to go to, why don't you go where fashion sits? Puttin' on the ritz."*

All at once, people around her were applauding and Brent was moving to the podium. Maryvonne brought her attention back into the room. Brent thanked Stan and then reached down into the box he had brought and picked up a copy of the hardcover book and held it up. "*Right Foot, Left Foot: Bipartisan Shoes for a Young America* is not just the name of my book, it's my personal motto in life." He nervously cleared his throat then continued, "And everyone has to have a motto. When I was in college, my motto used to be *I like beer*."

This was meant to be his opening joke, but it fell flat in the well-heeled room.

He looked a little sheepish, apologized for the bad joke, and then went on about how he was tired of all the arguing in politics and how everyone should just stop bickering and be cool. Things got better from there. He talked about the history of footwear while showing pictures from his book. The photos of the old shoes were gorgeous. Maybe twenty shoes were profiled in glossy color, with a few pages of descriptive text and simple sketches of the mechanics after each photo. He talked on assuredly, answering audience questions along the way. The crowd was pretty engaged. Maryvonne found the talk interesting but a bit shallow. She was not quite sure how he had managed to land a job at the prep school. But he certainly did have a lot of confidence.

Maryvonne turned in her seat when someone from the back asked a question about the family spats. It was the girl in the pink flip-flops. Maryvonne had not looked at her face when she initially looked at her flip flops, and now she saw it was Pixie Smithson who also worked at the prep school, but in the IT department. Brent replied that his Wickingham forebear in England, who was a distant cousin to the Duke of Cambridge, had invented spats and for decades first sold them to the military in all the European countries before they went mainstream. It was practically a monopoly for the first fifty years, then they went out of fashion after the Wall Street Crash.

Aha! Maryvonne deduced from this comment that he was a trust-fund kid with connections to people and schools in England. Perhaps that had translated into some connection in the prep school hiring office.

The talk ended and Brent took ten books out of his box and placed them on the signing table in two stacks.

He also produced a full-sized calendar from out of the box, set it on the table near the books, opened it to July and began making hash marks in one of its squares. Pixie Smithson came rushing to the front and was first in line, looking all moony at him. A small line began forming behind her.

Maryvonne moved toward the back and struck up a conversation with Stan about a new local literary trail walking map she had heard about. He went to get her one from among the promotional stacks near the cash register, and then said, "Oops, they are ..."

"...disparu," Effie said from behind the counter, finishing his sentence while ringing up a sale.

"Disparu," said Maryvonne. "Yes, missing - vanished - disappeared, very good! Not a very common word at all, your French must be really coming along, Effie. The Paris trip is coming up soon?"

"Oui," replied Effie. "Deux semaines, and we can't wait!" She went on, "Stan can you run down stairs and get some more Exeter Literary Trail maps…"

"...from the backstock," he finished her sentence. "Oui, ma chèrie," he cooed then headed towards the door practicing the word "disparu" over and over in a skat. Maryvonne left Effie to her work at the counter ringing up book sales, and sauntered to the back of the store to look out the large window at the river and the converted mills on the far side where many of her friends lived. When he returned Stan handed Effie the stack of slim tri-fold maps to fill the empty spot, then found Maryvonne at the back window and gave her one fresh copy.

"Enjoy your walk, Maryvonne," Stan said and moved away to service other patrons.

"Merci beaucoup," she said as she took the map in her hand. She glanced over it for a moment and then tucked it in her purse. Maryvonne headed towards the door, noticing that the line was now gone and that Brent had two copies still left on the desk. Pausing in the doorway she looked back to see Brent re-taping his big box of many remaining books and Stan coming towards him to square up accounts.

He carried that heavy thing all the way down here in such hopes, Maryvonne thought, feeling ambivalent as she stepped out into the night air. The darkness took hold of her - it had been a long day and she was ready for bed.

Chapter 5

There's a red house over yonder
That's where my baby stays

The heat was already coming on strong by the time Maryvonne awoke. Peering at the clock beside the bed, she couldn't believe what it said. How could it be nine already? Sliding out of the bed, she made her way towards the bathroom for her morning beauty rituals.

"Are you finally awake? You really slept a long time. How are you feeling? How's the bump?" Zeus called from the bottom of the stairs. She turned around and looked down at him from the top of the stairs, he was all dressed and chipper. She was feeling pretty chipper herself.

"I'm feeling great today," she called back. "That late sleep did me a world of good after the early rise yesterday. I barely notice the bump; it feels better and looks better too. You look like you're ready to go somewhere."

"Yes, it's Friday so it's men's walking group today. We're meeting on the steps of the town hall in fifteen minutes to decide our route for the day," he said, checking his watch. "Then after that I have an appointment in Portsmouth. I won't be back until well after lunch."

"Oh, yes yes yes. Oui oui oui, I forgot. Go have fun with the boys. But let's go to the festival tomorrow morning. I'd like to see the Declaration reading. Should be fun."

"It's a date!" he replied. "I've got to go now, but I left some blueberry muffins in a basket on the table for you."

"I adore you!" she said, blowing him a kiss, and off he went. She showered and dressed and was soon at the table with muffins and a hot cup of coffee, thinking about all the events of yesterday.

Tabitha, Rhoda, and Scipio all turned over in her mind, but she still couldn't quite make out what it was all about. She was failing to see something important and it was irking her. The festival area would be crowded with people setting up tents and cannons right now, so she couldn't go back to her tree by Joe Saints and investigate. She instead decided to go take a look at Tabitha's uncle Major John Gilman's house on Cass Street this morning, and spend some quiet time there sketching.

Due to the heat, the fact that it was a workday, and that the festival was being set up just blocks away down on the riverbank, the historic neighborhood on the hill at the corner of Green and Cass was deserted. Maryvonne left her hybrid parked on the corner. She took her small folding chair and big art bag and set off to find the modest Georgian Gambrel-roof house, with its historical marker affixed near the red front door, standing proudly at the far end of Cass Street near Park and Summer.

Trying to determine the most attractive angle to sketch it, she walked about it for a few moments. Across the narrow street on the grass fell the slim shade of a telephone pole. That felt right. She set up her chair knowing she was on someone's property, but the house seemed abandoned. It was wrapped in Tyvek insulation sheeting and the windows showed an empty interior. She positioned herself in the slice of shade so she wouldn't have to wear her hat, and have it press on her small bump, for now that she was walking around in the heat it did tingle occasionally.

Out of her bag she took a sketch pad, a small tin of Reeves drawing pencils in H's and B's, a gum eraser and her purple earbuds. She had already decided to put in the earbuds with no sound, to replicate as closely as possible the details from yesterday. She was going to try to copy the conditions that were in place just before her "vision" or whatever it was. Would anything happen? If it did, would it help her figure out anything? She didn't know if she was wasting her time, but she felt compelled to give it a try, and if nothing happened, well then c'est la vie.

After getting everything in order she sat back for a minute, to let all that prep-fuss fade away from her mind, and to get acclimated to the scene. Sipping slowly from her water bottle she started assessing the angles and tones. She would not have to deal with color today, as it would be a black and white sketch. Putting down the water, she picked up the 3H pencil and started.

Using a light touch with the pencil, she blocked in the house in relation to the tree and the white fence in front of it, which was overhung with a white rose vine. Something was off in the composition, so she had to use the eraser and start over. Sketching for her was more of a struggle than painting. Every detail had to be so fine, and sometimes it was hard for her to see the right tone and correlate it to the correct pencil. Hunkering down she had to really focus on the job at hand; it began to get easier, and she began to get in the flow. Fence, rose vine, clapboards. Looking up, looking down at the paper. Pressing harder now for a darker line, now softer for hash marks to shade. Two windows on each side, a central entrance flanked by pilasters and topped by a transom and a gabled pediment. Looking up, looking down. Pressing hard, pressing soft. In the flow now. One large granite front step. A red front door with three panels. Looking down. Looking up. She felt her mind slip its confines. The front door opened.

Tabby stepped out onto the large granite step with a battered black leather satchel in her hand. There was a long white ribbon tied in a bow on one of the handles. She carefully placed it on the step, leaning against the house, tucked slightly behind a long-stemmed red rose bush at the left side of the step. The door remained open and Maryvonne could see a few women in aprons rushing to and fro. Tabby was dressed in her finest today: a navy satin dress with gold trim. She had gold ribbons in her hair.

Maryvonne looked to see her shoes, but they were hidden under the skirt. *Dang*, she thought. Maryvonne was in full control of her mind, and had been waiting for this moment while she sketched. She was about to call out to Tabby when an older man came through the door, also dressed in sartorial splendor. He wore a cream satin waistcoat, federal blue breeches, and a black tri-corner hat trimmed in gold with a red cockade rosette. He was speaking.

"My dear niece Tabitha, I do owe you a debt for stepping in to hostess for me at this most important gathering while your aunt is ill and feeble. Tut-tut. Poor thing," said the grey-haired man in a slightly British accent. Tabitha did a silent curtsey in reply. The uncle sighed and went on in his clipped accent, "I must say, you do look quite fetching. The memory of your youthful visage will give us boys fortitude when the battles get rough, knowing that we are fighting for the freedom and happiness of our good and noble Gilman family."

While pulling down the waistcoat over his plump belly he continued, "I know that your father and I are a tad old for this type of endeavor, but nevertheless, we both served with courage during the Seven Years War with the French and Indians, and shall both put forward our names to the captain for this campaign." At that he straightened his hat and pulled it low over his brow while sticking out a determined chin.

"Yes uncle, you and father served quite admirably, as did Caesar," she replied.

"Caesar, yes. He is like a son to me. That is why he will be attending this, our final gathering of Gilman men, before those who are chosen march off to war. I am delighted to have him feast with us and plan strategy like we did in the old days." He looked up past Tabby. "Here comes Reverend Rumpole already, I am certain that his prayers and blessings at our gathering will ensure victory and safe return for our men."

Maryvonne saw the old Reverend hurry up to the house in a rather haphazard way, his robes crinkled and his stole askew. He threw up his hands, "Major, this is the day the Lord hath made!" he said to the sky by way of greeting the two. "Ah, Tabitha my lamb, you were gracious to shepherd the young songbird Rhoda to the town common yesterday to warble the lovely hymn after my prayer and blessing. Brought a tear to my eye, truth be told."

Tabby bowed as she said slowly and regally, "It was my honor and privilege, Reverend."

"War has been declared. Grave times may be ahead, my child, grave times. It is *my* honor and privilege to attend your ancestral feast and ask for the Lord to bless and favor this family. Forgive me, Major, I may get the exact words of the blessing a little mixed up since I have lost my satchel, once again, in which I carry my Bible, notes, and letters. Holy Heavens! As our French friends would say - it's disparu!" At this the Reverend took out a crumpled handkerchief from his robe pocket and mopped his brow with an exaggerated flourish and then continued, "This turn of events is quite an inconvenience. I did not know that John Taylor tucked the letter from Philadelphia inside my satchel as well, after he read it and the extraordinary commotion ensued," the overheated Reverend said, wringing his hands. "Your uncle Nicholas has me in sackcloth and ashes over it."

"Do not fret, Reverend, there is no disparu, your missing satchel is here," Tabby said calmly as she reached behind the bush and picked up the satchel, its white ribbon ends dragging across the red rose buds. "It had slipped off the Town House steps and Little Rhoda found it while searching for her bonnet. I tied this ribbon to it to help you to see it better in the future."

Reverend Rumpole went on in a state of joy clutching the satchel to his breast, admiring the ribbon. The uncle stood beside them, beaming at his niece. Maryvonne took it all in, including the French word "disparu."

All at once Maryvonne noticed a group of four dandily dressed men coming swiftly towards the house from one direction, and another solo man from the opposite.

"All arriving at once! My brothers Samuel and Nicholas, there you are with Nicholas Junior and John Taylor! I bid you hearty greetings!" The Major turned to the other side. "Caesar my friend! Greetings to you as well. Your little daughter sang like an angel yesterday!"

The group of men had now all reached the path to the front step and stopped, greeting one another. The Major took command, "Now we are all arrived. My sons are inside - they have been scribbling away all afternoon, making fixes and suggestions to ready our New Hampshire State Constitution for the coming victory. We have much to discuss, gentlemen. Come one, come all inside my humble home to feast as past and future men of valor," the Major chortled as he led them through the door.

Tabitha stood primly outside at the top of the step and nodded silently to each man in turn as they entered the house. Then she stood alone outside. Tabby swiveled her head and nodded to Maryvonne, and then Maryvonne could have sworn Tabby gave her... the fem-eye. Maryvonne's eyebrows shot up in surprise. Quickly, Tabby turned and delicately picked up her satin skirts, showing a bit of matching navy satin shoe, and stepped over the threshold and into the house. An aproned servant closed the door behind her.

Maryvonne sat very still, focusing on her third eye until she felt her mind quiveringly draw back. She was being asked to find something that was *disparu*. This she knew for certain, everything else was up for grabs.

Packing up the incomplete sketch, she hastily crossed the street to the sidewalk and headed back towards her car at the other end of Cass Street at a fast clip. She was halfway down the street when a shrill voice pierced her thoughts and stopped her in her tracks.

Someone was screaming like death. Then there was another angry voice shouting. And more screaming. She couldn't make out what they were saying, but it was not good. This apparent domestic violence incident seemed to be playing out in the backyard of the red house that sat behind a gracious magnolia tree. Maryvonne cautiously turned into the driveway, tip-toed to the far end and peeked around the back corner of the house to see if someone needed help.

There on a very large wooden back porch she saw Pixie Smithson. Pixie was a petite girl with short purple hair and flashing dark eyes. She was struggling with a large, elderly, sun-spotted man in a wheelchair, trying to take a grimy white tee shirt off him. He was screaming that he was being attacked. She was yelling, "Gramps, you stink, it's too hot to wear that shirt for a week." There was a clean tee-shirt folded on the picnic table beside them. In reply he spurted out a stream of foul swear words that made Maryvonne grimace.

Uncertain what to do, Maryvonne backed up a couple of steps in the driveway so they wouldn't see her. Not that they would have, they were fully engaged in the tussle. Maryvonne heard a big thump and Pixie groaned, "Gramps, don't push me like that for gossakes! I am only taking off your stinking shirt. At least I got it finally. Here, put on this clean one."

The stream of swears started up again. Pixie was no effing good, she was stealing effing money out of his effing tee shirt pocket, and she was ugly to boot.

Maryvonne heard the old man finish his tirade by spitting loudly on the porch.

"Every time! Damn old stinking coot, just shoot me if I get dementia like that. I am either his servant or his attacker. Man, what a life, I can't wait to get out of here," Maryvonne heard Pixie say softly, apparently to herself. Following that in a much louder voice Pixie said, "Gramps, my break is over, I am going back to the tech office now." Then it was very quiet. Maryvonne peeked again around the edge of the house to see the old man muttering and putting on the clean shirt alone, while a large screen curtain with magnetic closures was fluttering in the wind from Pixie's forceful entering into the back of the house. Maryvonne beat a hasty retreat up the driveway.

As soon as she got close to the top of the driveway though, she heard the front door slam and Pixie came rushing down the steps, and in a twinkling her pink flip-flops started beating a rhythm on the sidewalk. Maryvonne delayed until Pixie got some distance ahead, then stepped out onto the sidewalk as if nothing had happened and slowly walked the rest of the way to her parked car on Green Street.

Pixie continued walking down the hill and crossed the street, turned right and headed towards the prep school IT offices, two doors down from Joe Saints. Maryvonne got in her car at the top of the hill, and sped off silently under the pep of electric power. Thankfully, Pixie's grandfather was not her problem.

Chapter 6

I 'm tired of wasting all my precious time...
Foxy Lady

Disparu. Disparu. What could be missing? Perhaps something would come to her if she poked around Swasey Parkway. She had the afternoon free until her weekly get-together at yoga class with her friend Anjali. All day long groups of people would be setting up the bulk of the festival along the riverside park. The festival was representative of Tabitha's era, so Maryvonne might be able to glean some clues.

Parking would be tough already down by the river, so she would park on a side street further in town. She steered the car down Tan Lane, a small one-way street that went through the heart of the prep school's art and science campus buildings. It must have been a class change, so many young summer school students were crossing the street, their full backpacks pressing the weight of the world onto their slim shoulders. Maryvonne had to wait. She tapped her nails on the steering wheel and wondered how to find a something that was missing when she didn't know what it was in the first place.

A small Asian boy was carrying a very large cello case across the road in front of her, heading towards the music center. At the curb he bumped the case and it opened slightly, the gap allowing sheets of paper to cascade onto the sidewalk and into the street. She waited longer and thought some more, while he retrieved his music. She still could not come up with any good ideas; she would just have to walk about and trust her intuition.

The street cleared and she drove to the end and took a left, then another left after the campus green to circle back towards the parkway. She found a parking spot near the campus store, took her purse and got out of the car. Standing alongside the car she locked it with the fob, took a deep breath and let it out sharply. "Allons!" she said firmly, and marched off towards the riverbank that was the reason why the town existed in the first place.

The scene on Swasey Parkway along the river was quite the hullabaloo already. Everything would have to be in place tonight to greet the attendees when they started swarming in on Saturday morning. Today was the day of transforming the riverbank into tomorrow's time warp of the summer of 1776. Maryvonne looked around at the heaps of stuff being hauled about by people and pickup trucks and trailers: white canvas tents, iron kettles and anvils, muskets, cannons. Military encampments were slowly beginning to take shape. Some of the "soldiers" would be spending the night in their simple white tents.

And this year a lacuna that had been brushed aside for years would be finally filled - a mostly Black militia encampment would also be set up, similar to Varnum's Regiment, in an effort to acknowledge Black contributions. The Museum had hired a new director eleven months ago, Bella Volpe, an intelligent and fashionable young red-headed woman who was resolute in telling the whole truth of the birth of America, not just a few white-washed stories.

Under Bella's watch, an important gap in telling the story of Exeter's role in the creation of a "United States" of America would be filled in. Maryvonne made a note to come back the following day to see how Jude Hall would be represented in an encampment for the first time. Since talking with the Brim about Jude's story, she had continued to try to sort through feelings she couldn't even name quite yet.

Maryvonne looked and looked and found nothing in the way of leads or serendipity. Disappointed that the parkway did not yield anything that prickled her mind, she turned away and headed back out onto the main street and to the spot where she had been painting yesterday near the glass-fronted building. She stood under the chokecherry tree and looked about as the people rushed to and fro around her. There was nothing special about this place either. She went to peer into the door that she had last seen Scipio's shadow pass through, but all she saw was her reflection in the unwashed glass.

Leaning her back against the building, she sighed and closed her eyes. Maybe she was trying too hard. She decided to practice a small meditation technique she often used to slow herself down: ten slow breaths while repeating her mantra in rhythm. "Calm, sure, orgasmagical...calm, sure, orgasmagical..." The mantra rose and fell like gentle waves on a warm, sparkling ocean. It was very relaxing. After the tenth repetition she opened her eyes. They leisurely focused on the stone wall across the street, then sharply focused on the plastic compost bin atop it. She felt compelled to walk across the street and look at it once again.

When she got there though, it was not the compost bin she found compelling, but the square cut in the grass below her feet. She stooped down to investigate. Doubting that anyone would notice what she was doing since they were all across the street doing things themselves, she pulled a pen out of her purse and stuck it into the slit closest to her. Slowly she pried up an edge of the square sod. She managed to get up enough of one corner to get a good grasp on the edge and peel the whole thing back. It flopped upside down in one piece on the grass. Under was nothing but dirt, firmly packed.

Again using the pen, she stabbed into the dirt square a number of times to see if it hit upon anything. Nothing. Hmmm. She lifted up the sod square and flopped it back down into place, then stepped on it a few times to make sure it was completely returned to the way she found it. Good. Only a small sprinkling of dirt remained, marking the area on the grass where the flipped piece had been.

Brushing her hands on her jeans, she stood up and looked about. All was still quiet in the backyard of the

Folsom Tavern. Walking along the edge of the wall from left to right she found no other cuts in the grass. The newspaper story had mentioned that ten sample pits were dug on the compound. Perhaps there would be more by the house. Her eyes scanned over the grass, looking here and there for any sign of a square cut. Off to one side of the back door near the nook formed by the old lilac bushes she found one.

This cut was much larger, perhaps three or four feet square, and a terra cotta pot of red impatiens sat atop of it in the center. Maryvonne squatted down with her back almost touching the shady bushes where they met the tavern. She dragged the flower pot off to one side and inspected the cut. This cut was not as clean as the other. Taking her pen, she pried up an edge and it came up easily. Rolling it back three-quarters of the way she plunged her pen in the dirt several times.

Although it went in quite easily as compared to the other square, she still came up empty. Sitting back on her haunches she stared at the dirt and let her mind wander for a minute. She didn't even know what she was looking for anyway. Was she expecting to hit "pay dirt" right away? What a laugh. Maybe she never would and this was all a big farce. She frowned and began rolling the sod back in place. She was just reaching for the flower pot when she heard the back-door lock click. Feeling like a fool squatting on the ground, she pressed herself back into the shady nook of the many leaves and hoped whoever it was would not notice her.

The door opened and she heard talking. "I'll be right back; I'm just running up the hill to my office to get the cash box and roll of raffle tickets so we can have that all set for tomorrow morning." One shapely leg ending with red toenails peeping out of a red patent strappy Italian Ferragamo wedge sandal set down on the step, then a crash came from somewhere inside the building, and the leg slipped back in the building. Maryvonne recognized those fantastic shoes.

"What on earth was that?" called Bella loudly.

"This vase tipped over," came a muffled reply from inside.

Footsteps came close to the door and suddenly a hand stuck out with a half-broken glass flower vase and dumped the remaining water on the step, and disappeared inside. The door stood open.

"That was so odd, I don't think I bumped it, I wasn't even close enough. I was looking at the Dunlap and turned around and the roses were all over the floor. I don't know how it happened," said a soft male voice.

"And you know what is even more odd?" continued the soft voice. "I am just a volunteer and might be imagining this, but something seems off with the frame of the Dunlap."

Bella gave a nervous laugh and said, "Really, Spencer, that is just silly. How could that possibly be true?" She laughed again, more of a manic whinny really, then continued, "It's probably just the way it's displayed this year with that blue light seeping everywhere and those silver stars sparkling all around. Those professional window dressers really outdid themselves with the display case this year."

"Come over here and look at it with me," said Spencer's soft voice, and Maryvonne heard them both moving inside, so she quickly dragged the flower pot back over the sod and stood up. Pressing against the building, she moved closer to the door, straining to hear the conversation. "It's the frame. I could have sworn it had a small scuff on this bottom edge in the shape of a dog bone. I saw the dog bone on Wednesday at the end of the day when I locked up. But I didn't see it yesterday when I took my lunch break, and I don't see it now. I'm sorry I didn't say anything yesterday, Bella."

Bella laughed nervously again. "I think you are imagining things, Spencer. How could anything happen to the document when there is a security camera right on it, and at all the doors?"

It was then that Maryvonne glanced up and saw the small security camera above the door. "Mon Dieu," she exclaimed harshly under her breath as her attention was drawn to the camera. She was sure her whole flowerpot and digging incident had been caught on camera, and it would be embarrassing. As would this leaning into the doorway to listen. She rolled her eyes and berated herself. But then the conversation inside continued, and teased Maryvonne's attention away from her own stupidity and back inside the tavern. "I think you should have it checked out," said Spencer.

A very strident tone hissed in reply, "And have them think I am a neurotic woman? No way. This is my first time running the festival weekend and I don't want any problems. Everything is fine." Then in a more indulgent tone Bella said, "Spencer, I insist that you forget about it. Everything is fine. I promise. Now not another word about it."

Maryvonne sensed the conversation was ending, so she backed up several yards along the wall and slipped away into the small opening where the old bush met the building. Quickly she skittered across the small parking lot to the sidewalk.

Making her way back to her car she was overcome with the feeling that the 1776 Dunlap Broadside in the display case was indeed a fraud. The knowing washed over her like a cold rain. Then the questions came. Why would she be picked to know this secret? What to do about it anyway? Go to the police and tell them. Yes! But no! Where is the proof? She would appear a nutcase. Maryvonne felt overwhelmed. Thankfully, it was almost time to meet Anjali at Yogasmyth - and she was so glad.

After the day she had had, the thing she wanted to do most was to empty her mind, and yoga class was one of the best places to do just that. She shifted her car into drive, cranked up the radio volume just as Jimi bellowed, *"You make me want to get up and a-scream!"* and zoomed home to change.

Chapter 7

They don't realize
They're the ones who square
...cuz I'm stone free

Forty-five minutes later she was dressed in her yoga pants, stretchy top, little black flip-flops with crushed rhinestones across the band, and was climbing the staircase to the yoga studio atop the shops on the main drag. Anjali was already in the dressing room looking for her mat in the cubbies. Maryvonne entered and kicked off her shoes, tucked her car keys inside them, and greeted her, "Hello Anjali, how are you?"

"M.V.! Hey girlfriend, I missed you last week!" Anjali exclaimed warmly back. "Are you feeling better?"

"Much better. I would say I'm 95% recovered."

"Great. Do you have time for a walk after class? Let's get an iced coffee and take a walk over to the bench."

"That sounds great!" Maryvonne replied enthusiastically as they headed out of the dressing room and into the large and bright studio space for an hour of yoga. The room was already crowded so they separated and put their mats down at opposite ends of the room. Maryvonne curled into the yogic "child's pose" with her forehead on the mat and let the day begin to seep out of her head and into the ground.

This particular class was Maryvonne's favorite offering of the week at the studio. The instructor John, a young man of Polish descent, taught a rasamaya-style class and focused each month on a different chakra, or energy center. This month the classes were dedicated to the solar plexus, located in the abdomen, which John described as the location of willpower. She hoped the class would help her re-boot her mind, so she could see more clearly.

Settling in, he began the class with his usual hand gestures, or mudras, and one big and long Om. The strong and clear sound of the Om cut through the fog in Mayvonne's mind and pulled it to focus on the task at hand. Puffing through the more difficult poses, like boat, Maryvonne was able to clear her mind and focus on her body for most of the hour. There were a few times when her mind slipped back into thinking about her to-do list, or glanced over in amazement at Anjali's perfectly executed poses, but mostly she managed to keep it free of serious thought. Maryvonne felt wonderfully refreshed in both body and mind when the final rest of savasana, or corpse pose, was completed and the class joined in unison for the closing "Namaste."

After the class Anjali and Maryvonne walked down the stairs together out into the brilliant sun of the hot day, parted to stow their yoga mats in their roasting cars, then met up again in the line at D-Java Hut for the iced coffees. Soon they were walking side-by-side on the sidewalk, happily sipping the icy goodness from their sweating cups, and catching up on their family news.

Anjali was a fit brunette who was married and had two girls in college. She worked part-time in the business office of a local church, and was a very spiritual woman - although not in the religious sense. She knew about herbs and goddesses and various earth-arts, and had a great sense of the serendipitous. Maryvonne thought of Anjali as an everyday wise-woman, as very little seemed to shake her and she had a great sense of fairness. She often had interesting stories to tell about the social justice projects the church was working on, so Maryvonne wanted to ask her thoughts on the racial history of Exeter when they got to the bench.

The two friends walked past the entrance to the busy parkway, past Joe Saints, past the summer school office, and then curved around the corner past the tech office and a children's daycare center. They crossed toward the corner of Green Street and headed up a small brick pathway lined with multi-trunked birch trees under which piles of dark green ivy tumbled down a shady embankment. At the top of this short, inclined path was a pretty pocket-park in a space that was once the Exeter Gas Works. Before that it was the location of one of the very first churches in town, because it was so close to the river and the small falls that caused Reverend John Wheelwright to found the town in 1638, after "purchasing" it from the natives.

Having caught up on family news, they sat down on one of the black metal benches set upon a starburst of paving stones fringed in the lush ivy, and faced themselves towards the river. Their frontmost view was mostly blocked by a large brick apartment building, but they could see some comings and goings of the continuing festival set up on the far side of the apartments. A series of small fruit trees in front of them provided flecks of shade.

Behind them the paved path continued into a small burial ground, once associated with the early church. It consisted of a few broken headstones and a large brick and cement tomb for Rev. Samuel Dudley, who died in 1683 according to the well-worn bronze plaque. This silent grouping of stones stood in the shade of a patch of unkempt woods surrounding it. The shadiness under this tiny grove afforded the two friends a slight cooling breeze occasionally wafting from that direction.

The starburst cement formed sort of a courtyard within the trees and was set with beautiful plantings that turned their faces towards the late afternoon sun. "C'est bon!" Maryvonne exclaimed and stood up to go look at an especially lovely blue hydrangea. "I have been thinking of painting a hydrangea and this plant is gorgeous. I have to take a picture." She fumbled around in her purse until she found her cell phone. Getting very close to the showy bloom she tapped on the center of her touch screen to bring the flower into sharp focus, which made the leaves in the background slightly blurry. "Magnifique - that is a charming composition, it will make a great painting."

Happy with the shot, she sat back down on the bench and showed it to Anjali, who nodded in approval. Maryvonne went to slip the cell phone back in her purse when she upset her iced coffee and managed to grab the slippery cup quickly before the purse got wet. Maryvonne took a long sip of her drink and finished it off before she could make any other messes.

"Now," she said to Anjali, "I want to ask your opinion on something, mon amie." She did not want to mention her story of the visions to anyone quite yet, just the underpinnings of it.

Anjali pulled the elastic out of her ponytail and let her long brown hair fall free onto her shoulders. "Sure M.V., I am honored that you would ask my humble opinion. Please, go on." Her dusky blue eyes looked merrily into Maryvonne's green ones as she waited for the question.

"Well, there has been much talk recently about the Black community in Exeter that thrived just after the Revolutionary War," Maryvonne began.

"Yes, I have seen some recent stories in the news highlighting it and our racial history. I must admit I was quite surprised to find out this town had the highest percentage of Black citizens in the state at that time. What was it? Something like eighty free Blacks and two thousand whites? That figure was shocking to me. I thought this persnickety white town had always been white."

"Me too, Anjali. I couldn't believe how those families were all but run out of town after about thirty or forty years' time, despite all they contributed to the founding of the country. And did you read the full story of the escaped slave turned soldier, Jude Hall?"

"Yes." Anjali's blue eyes had taken on a serious look now.

"And how do you feel about the tragedy at Jude's Pond on Drinkwater Road?"

"Short reply? Angry and embarrassed. And also confused," came the reply.

"Please go on, give me the long reply," said Maryvonne as she leaned back into the bench. The luscious late afternoon sun shone upon Maryvonne's upturned face, and wrapped both women and the bench in a curious glow, set off against the darkness of the small shady grove behind them

Anjali drained the last few sips of her drink, looking down at her tanned hands while gathering her thoughts, then began, "M.V., you know I live on Drinkwater Road on the way to Jude's Pond. Ever since I read that ugly story of the kidnapping of Jude's teenaged son James from his mom's house, I can't stop feeling that I have been duped."

Anjali looked away for a moment then began again, "Feeling duped is what makes me initially angry, then embarrassed. Angry that I had always been taught that crazy stuff like that happened in the South and that Northerners like me had no connection at all to the institution of slavery. Angry that the alleged crime was perpetrated by another Exeter citizen. Angry that the town fathers or town at large took no action. Angry that it did not even make the news and there is no paper trail whatsoever, save one deposition and one article in Boston decades later."

She paused, and thought for another moment before she went on, "But my anger is inconsequential in the face of the anger of the people that had to put up with horrible treatment like that for hundreds of years, even until today, so I feel like my anger doesn't really count. Or maybe should not even be spoken about. How can it possibly compare?"

Anjali was looking off into the distance now as she spoke and the pace of her words quickened. "And I also said I was embarrassed. This embarrassment, although initially because of feeling duped by history, turns to something deeper. I admit, M.V., this is not the first time

I've heard stories like this, but I must say it's the first time I've actually *heard.*"

Anjali was going on like a freight train now as one thought was articulated after another, her voice growing tense. "And why the change in hearing? Why now? Simple answer: even though it was over two hundred years ago, this tragedy happened on the street where I live. I find that surreal! And here comes that anger again. A secondary feeling of anger - at myself now - because it took the fact of *proximity* to make me *hear*... if that makes any sense."

She shook her head and her voice went back to its normal tone. "The truth is there are a whole lot of confused feelings for me around this story, and the larger story of the near extinction of the entire Black community of Exeter as well. I don't even know what to think."

Anjali paused and crossed both hands over her heart. "But then all the anger turns to grief when I think of Rhoda. Or maybe compassion. She never really is the focus of the story, but I identify with her the most. My children and I walk my street in the same exact footsteps as that family. Can you imagine the sorrow of Rhoda, how heavy her heart was as she trudged that lonely, wooded street back and forth to town alone, knowing that her baby had been sold into slavery? Wondering where he was, how he was, if he was still alive?"

Maryvonne furrowed her eyebrows and shook her head, but remained silent.

Anjali hung her head dismally and went on, hands still clasped at her heart. "Rhoda fought the intruder, but he grabbed her son right out of her arms." Anjali looked up into Maryvonne's eyes, "Can you imagine that happening to you? I think of my own children."

She paused for a moment with furrowed brows. "It breaks my heart to know that poor family was purposely…" here she searched about for the right word and then said, "*...sundered.*"

Anjali let her hands drop from her heart onto her lap and continued, "It appears the town did nothing about it, but who knows? Maybe the citizens that were horrified about it were too afraid to speak out against the bullies of the time." Then she went on, "Given all that Jude did - for eight years he fought in the war under the same flag as their husbands and sons - it seems despicably unfair. It is a complete moral breach, bullies or not."

Sensing a break in her thoughts Maryvonne leaned forward and interjected, "So bottom line, where does it stand for you now?"

Anjali stared at her for a brief moment then blinked and said firmly, "The whole grievous affair is soul-crushing and there is some very bad karma that needs to be transmuted. Not only with Jude and Rhoda's story, but the truth about what happened to the entire Black community in Exeter needs to be officially addressed. It's just going to fester until then."

"Namaste my friend," responded Maryvonne, with a slight bow. "How do you see it being addressed?"

Anjali shifted in her seat and folded her arms on her lap. "I don't really know. Seems tricky because taking someone's voice by appropriation is never a good thing. But who will speak when no one is left? Who has the right to reclaim lost voices like that?"

"Seems like the American Independence Museum is speaking, for one," replied Maryvonne. "They are giving Jude back his rightful place in the town's history this weekend."

"Yes, I suppose," Anjali replied, "and the Historical Society held a public reading of Frederick Douglass's Fourth of July speech a couple of weeks ago. It was well attended. I went and got assigned a paragraph to read along with about thirty others from around town."

Anjali put her hand to her chin and looked off into the distance. "It was a powerful speech. And really weird to hear his words coming out of the mouths of various white people I know. That was a kind of transmutation. Although maybe it comes more under the heading of Preaching to the Choir."

Her thoughts shifted and she went on, "But again, who speaks for Rhoda? The paper trail for her and most women of that time virtually does not exist. Yes, it's surely a conundrum. Many minds need to thresh through this to find the correct answer."

Looking at her watch, Anjali shifted her thoughts again, "Sorry, both of my girls are home on summer break and I don't get to see them much anymore. I promised them a nice family dinner tonight, and I have to start cooking soon so let's head back now."

Anjali dipped her hand into her purse and retrieved her elastic scrunchie and began tying her loosened hair back again. "So M.V., why did you want to know my thoughts on Jude Hall and his Black Exeter community?"

Maryvonne hesitated and then chose her words carefully. "Among other things, I was down at the festival set-up earlier today and was thinking about Jude and Rhoda and the fact that there is a lacuna in Exeter's town record, as you just mentioned. The missing story is so awkward, and I am so confused by it too. I could not even articulate my feelings to myself. Anjali, I thank you for being so frank. It has helped me. Namaste, my friend." Maryvonne gave a flourishing bow with her hands clasped in front of her.

"Now Anjali, you know I am a woman of action, but I am not sure what, if anything, to do. And truthfully, so much time has passed, could any redress make a difference? Even just an apology? I tend to think so. But I don't even know where to start. I have to incubate this for a while and see what doors open. I am sure there are already local entities working on this. I think there is an organization in Portsmouth. Yes. Seems that I have some homework to do."

Maryvonne picked up her purse and got up to leave, when her feet caused her iced coffee cup to upend again and the last of the melted ice cubes to slosh onto her shoes and drip down into the ivy. "Again? Seriously. I didn't know I could be so clumsy."

Anjali chuckled and said, "Maybe it's the karma gods, what have you been up to lately?"

Picking up the empty cup and shaking out the last drops Maryvonne laughed and said, "You don't want to know!" She wasn't ready to tell her friend about the snooping around yet. Maryvonne knew herself to be prone to behaviors that others saw as odd. She preferred to think of it as adventurous.

The two friends headed swiftly back down the small path and across the street, towards their separate evenings. The corner of Water Street marked the halfway point to their cars, and Maryvonne and Anjali parted ways. Maryvonne did not want to go home yet: she wanted to sit and sort out things alone.

On the corner where Maryvonne stopped was a small grassy area where a few years back had stood a small rickety white house. The day the house was torn down by a backhoe, she had been walking by and paused to witness its demise. The sight that day of the yellow backhoe ripping into the roof and crushing the building down to the ground had made her feel melancholy. Often, she remembered that feeling when she passed by the small park that now stood there.

Maryvonne seated herself on a picnic table under a tree as she mused about the ephemeral quality of life. Even this park would not be a park forever. If her memory served her, the whole parcel of four other old buildings on this corner were all owned by the prep school, and some other configuration might soon seem important. But today it was a quiet park with three benches, a picnic table, and two curving paths that led to the entrance of the summer program offices of the prep school.

Fingers tapping on the table, she sat staring into space, mudlarking around in her mind about the events of yesterday and today. Piecing events together, she came up with this sequence: While engaged in art-flow, she had seen visions of Exeter in 1776. She had gotten the message that something from the Revolutionary era was missing. The Dunlap copy of the Declaration of Independence could be that thing. If it was indeed, it would seem the heist took place between Wednesday night and Thursday noon.

Now she set herself to consider who would do it, why and how?

It came to her that she had set up her easel quite early on Thursday morning across from the Folsom tavern and had been transported to 1776. The memory of that vision and the second one had commanded her full attention for almost two days. But now she thought back to the exact sequence earlier that day, before she looked up to see Tabitha and Rhoda crossing the street. Yes, Maryvonne had seen several real people that early morning before she saw Tabby.

Her fingers moved on the table again as if they were sliding beads around on an invisible abacus: While still driving in her car, she had seen a woman in white pants run across the street strangely. Then she had seen Joe the baker trot across the street with a large bag of baguettes. After that she saw Brent Wickingham cutting through the backyard of the tavern on his way to get coffee. None of these individuals had seen her. Could the thief be one of them? She had also heard Bella insist that

Spencer not mention his hunch to anyone. Could it be Bella herself? Or an inside job by someone else associated with the museum?

Now, why would they do it? If the thief were able to sell the piece on the black market, they would get a whole lot of money. That was pretty clear. Millions. How long did it take to get a buyer for something like that? How would the thief get it out of town to a buyer or a middle man? She wondered if the person who did it would leave town for good. If someone suddenly left town, that would be suspicious. Yes. Stan and Effie were going to Paris shortly; could they be added to the list ...or was she just grasping at straws now? Maryvonne felt out of her depth. It occurred to her that television scripts had taken possession of her line of thought. She wrinkled her nose and let out a sigh.

What to do? She supposed she could talk to some of these people and feel them out. The only person she really knew was Joe, and the bakery was already closed for the day. She would chat him up tomorrow morning. She could also talk to Bella, but she doubted she would get anywhere, given that Bella had already squelched Spencer. Maybe Spencer had some ideas. She didn’t really know Brent, but she did know he was leaving town for summer break. But that wasn’t unusual for teachers. And lastly, she didn't even know the name of the woman in white pants who had run across the street, but she thought she might be the new director of the summer school.

On to how. It was a mystery to Maryvonne as to how something could be stolen while in a locked case in a locked room, with security cameras in use. Her mind went back to the possibility of an inside job. Then she thought that perhaps she was lacking in imagination. She herself would be a pretty poor thief apparently. She snorted out loud at the thought.

She really had no idea if the Dunlap in the case had been replaced or not, and would not be able to find out on her own. She had seen it in past years and it just looked like a piece of old parchment paper the size of a small poster inside a special glass frame with a black metal edge. She guessed it must be some special archival frame with a preserving gas in between the panes. It didn't seem as if it would be too heavy, or too large to move around easily.

Suddenly she remembered that Thursday morning she had seen two people going across the street holding things that could have actually held something the size of the frame: the woman with her flat box, and Joe with his oversized bag of baguettes. Well that was something.

Reaching a dead end with her thoughts, and belly starting to rumble, she was ready to go home and cook dinner with Zeus. Looking towards the street, she saw that the commuter traffic was picking up. The workday was ending and the blazing sun was getting low. Just then, in the distance the back door to the summer school office swung open and several people came out, the last person turning to lock the door. Maryvonne looked in their direction as she began to stand up to leave. The first people out the door were a couple of young students who said goodbye to the two older women who were still on the steps, and then headed off towards the dorms.

"Maryvonne, is that you?" Maryvonne squinted towards the woman who was coming down the steps alone, and it took a moment for her to realize it was her friend Anne. Anne and Zeus had shared time in the science department before he retired and both families had become close friends. Anne and her young family had dined at their house many times and vice versa.

"Maryvonne, is that you?" Anne said again. "How are you?"

"Bien, Anne. Great to see you!" Maryvonne strode towards Anne and gave her a big hug. "How's the new house coming along? Are you keeping up with the dead-heading of the lilies?" Anne and her husband had recently bought a house on a large wooded lot on the edges of town.

Anne laughed, "No, they've gotten the best of me. I've given up. Too many other things to do this first year. You two will have to come over for dinner soon, now that we have the kitchen all set up."

The other woman had finished locking the door, spritely descended the steps, and now caught up with Anne on the path. "Maryvonne," Anne continued "this is my friend Adeola, who runs the summer program. Adeola, this is Maryvonne. I was telling you the other day about her colorful paintings."

"Nice to meet you," Adeola said with a big smile as she reached out her hand. Maryvonne shook hands with the beautiful and slim dark-skinned woman with her long braids piled atop her head like a crown. "You can call me Addie. I didn't quite get your name, I am sorry. It was Mary…?"

"Maryvonne, like Mary and Yvonne combined. Very French," she replied and shook hands, while realizing that Addie was probably the woman in the white pants from yesterday. "Likewise, Addie. Nice to meet you, I think I saw you early yesterday morning running across the street with a big, flat box." The words fell out of Maryvonne's mouth before she even had time to censor them.

A hint of mortification passed over Addie's face and she grimaced playfully. "You saw that? My God, it was so early, I was hoping no one did!"

This strange exclamation caused both women to stare at Addie questioningly. "What are you talking about?" said Anne. "That is a very interesting comment."

Addie started out slowly, "Well you know what always seems to happen when you are wearing white pants? It happened while I was walking into the office from my apartment early yesterday morning. A complete surprise. I felt a big splat when I was just across the street there." She motioned across the street to the sidewalk on the far side.

"Good Lord!" said Anne at the same time Maryvonne said "Mon Dieu!" and they both giggled, for women know of these things instinctively.

"Luckily, I was carrying this big, flat box of poster-sized easel pads, so I was able to hold it behind me and avert too much of a scene with the bakers and breakfast staff at the school kitchen over there," she said chagrined, pointing at the brick and smoked glass building across the intersection. "I got myself under control in my office then wrapped an extra sweater around my waist and went home to change."

"We've all been there," said Maryvonne. "That's a classic women's situation and you handled it well. I didn't notice anything of that nature."

Addie gave her the fem-eye in reply, then tossed her head back in laughter. "Why thank you. But I'm sorry that your first impression of me is so odd. We must all have a glass of wine one night and then you two can tell me your stories of the unexpected."

"I think that would be fun - I can think of one right now that is quite hilarious," Anne giggled. "The contortions we go through! My new house would be the perfect place to tell you the story - it has a really great private patio in the back. I'll send you both an email and we can pick a time soon." Anne said graciously.

"Magnifique!" replied Maryvonne. "Count me in! I have a couple of funny stories as well and I'll bring a bottle of Beaujolais."

"Great. It was nice to meet you, Maryvonne, and I'll see you again very soon," Addie pronounced, smiling broadly as they parted.

Chapter 8

Purple haze...
Whatever it is, that girl put a spell on me

Maryvonne and Zeus often took their summer cocktails in their side yard on the large wooden swing under the grape arbor which faced their rose garden. Maryvonne was in and out of the yard, setting up, and gloried in how it was scented with summer in the still air today. The golden dog slept contentedly in a crescent of shade under the lilac bush. Zeus was in the kitchen making two of his special Tequila-Lime Fizz drinks. A tray of herbed chicken breasts was roasting in the oven, and a green salad was chilling in the fridge. Maryvonne set her tablet to a jazz station, plugged in some speakers and turned them towards the open window, then went back outside to the garden.

She bounced backwards onto the green swing seat, making it sway. Slipping out of her flip flops, she pulled her tanned legs up, crossed them under herself and enjoyed the gentle ride. Soon, Zeus came out carrying the two frosty cocktails, set them on the small side table in the shade, and sat down heavily during the swing's up-motion. Roses and tall phlox lined the white picket fence, and the low sun was shining in their eyes despite the shade of the thick grape leaves. They swung on in silence, enjoying the buzzing and blooming view, until the swing stopped.

In the stillness, Zeus handed Maryvonne one of the chilly glasses. "Hooray for another day!" he toasted contentedly, while they clinked glasses.

"Now, my dear, what is this news you wanted to talk about?" he asked. Atop the limey drink in his hand were tiny specks of fizz, exploding into the late day sun. Maryvonne looked at the fizz, then dropped her bomb.

"I think the museum's copy of the Declaration of Independence may have been stolen."

"What...?" He gave her a curious look of disbelief. "Why do you think that? Wouldn't it be on the news if that were the case?"

"It has not been announced to the public yet," Maryvonne replied, looking into his questioning eyes, "and it may not be for some time, as it looks just as if nothing has happened."

"What on earth are you talking about? I don't follow you," he said, leaning over to put his drink back down on the shady side table and kicking off his shoes before picking the sweating glass up again and turning towards her.

"I overheard a conversation between the museum director Bella and a young male employee. He thinks the one in the display case is a fraud. And she tried to convince him otherwise, and then abruptly ended the conversation by making him swear he would not mention it again."

"And from that you are convinced it's a fraud? Seems like slim evidence," he said skeptically.

"Well, yes, I agree but I just have a hunch that something is off. The young man seemed to think that it was replaced sometime between Wednesday when he locked up and Thursday morning when he opened. And you know I was down there painting very early on Thursday morning," Maryvonne replied while wiping the condensation off her sweating glass and drying her hands on her shorts. "I saw three people dash out from behind that building at different times. All of them were acting quite odd."

"Oh, so now you are some kind of sleuth? I see," Zeus chortled as he took a long sip of his fizzy cocktail. "Tell me what you saw, and I will make my guess. You know I love a good puzzle."

"Oh mon chéri, even though you are not taking this seriously, I still adore you," she said and wrapped her arm around his shoulder to give him a quick hug. "Actually, I already have determined that one of the three has no involvement."

"Please tell me you are *not* going around town accusing people!" He looked serious. "I don't want anything to happen to you. There are a lot of weirdos out there."

"No, nothing like that. One of the people I saw was a woman that turned out to be a friend of Anne's. They were walking together and Anne introduced us. Through the course of normal conversation, she explained why she acted so oddly."

"And why was she acting odd?" he inquired.

"Sorry, I can't tell you. It's TMI," she replied, giving him the reverse fem-eye, the kind meant for men when they are poking around too much into the feminine mystique. "Let's just say she is off the list."

"Good grief," he grimaced and ground his teeth. "Ok, fine, I'll just let that one go. Now what about the other two?"

"I would say it's three, because the museum director Bella seemed quite suspicious when she told her employee to zip it. She was quite nervous and forceful. I don't trust her."

"Dare I ask how you overheard this conversation?

"Well, I was interested in the test pits the archeologists dug on the grounds last week. So I was poking around in one near the building when the two of them started talking. They didn't see me."

"I am not even going to ask why you were poking in test pits. However, I do believe that building has security cameras. And furthermore, your digging was probably captured on film, and come to think of it the camera would have captured the so-called heist."

"Correct on both. Let's just ignore my film debut, thank you for reminding me, and speak of the heist. It's clear it would be filmed. So why wouldn't Bella just say she was going to check out the film, instead of intimidating the kid to be silent? If she switched out the Dunlap inside those twelve or so overnight hours, it seems she would have been caught on camera too. But I would think maybe she has enough access to the security cameras to turn them off for five minutes, then switch them back on."

"An inside job."

"Yes. I always thought she was a clever woman in hot shoes, but now I wonder if she could be too clever."

"Ok, so she is suspect one in this game. Who are the other two? Did you recognize them?"

"Yes, I did. One was Joe the baker, and the other was Brent from the history department at the school."

"Oh jeez, the plot thickens."

"And did you realize that Stan and Effie from the bookstore are going to Paris next week? Seems like a good place to sell off a valuable document." Maryvonne wiped her wet hands on her shorts again and took a few long sips of the drink to help it stop sweating so copiously, then added, "I am not convinced yet that they should be added to the list, but I'm keeping my eyes and ears open."

"That seems a very scant chance; besides, they don't strike me as tech-savvy people who can manipulate a security camera," Zeus replied skeptically. "And why would they do it? Obviously, anyone stealing a rare document is most likely in it for the money. They seem to be doing fine and enjoying running the store."

"Stan is forever talking about retiring to Greece and just breezing from one jazz festival to the next. How many times have you heard him talk about the annual festival in Athens or Santorini, or some of the other islands? Effie has Greek heritage, it could work. If they retire shortly and head to Greece, then they are moving way up on my perp list." Maryvonne giggled then sighed, "Drifting around Greece actually sounds pretty good to me too."

"Let's move on before you get any big ideas. What about Joe and Brent? What did you see that morning?"

"Well I saw Joe first. He suddenly came out of nowhere, running across the street and carrying a large bag. I mean a large one, big enough to fit that document in its frame. The bag was full of baguettes, it would seem. He was looking around furtively, as if to make sure no one saw him, or he wasn't being followed or something. I wasn't paying too much attention, but I am pretty sure he didn't see me. I was in the shade and half behind a cement column. He ran across the street and then along the far side of his bakery. He probably went in the back door or to his car. I saw him in the kitchen when I got my coffee about thirty minutes later."

"So, you think he had the stolen document in the bag, and the baguettes were a decoy? Again, how is he getting by the camera?"

"You know that Joe is a birder and pretty darn good with cameras and video. He is always showing photos and videos to anyone who will talk birds with him. I have seen enough of his thrush and warbler videos to last a lifetime. He is no slouch when it comes to visual technology, always getting the latest gadgets. Perhaps he knows how to hack into a camera system."

"Ok, so we keep Joe high on the list. And Brent? If it was the dear boy, we could make it into that English crime show on PBS where the perp always turns out to be a professor from Oxford." Zeus had finished his cocktail and was getting more jovial in tone, "Oxford would seem to be loaded with oddball criminals. I wonder who does the hiring there, and if Brent could turn out to be one of those hires here in Exeter?"

"Mon chéri, are you saying that the local prep school could be staffed with oddballs? Did that include yourself?" She herself only had ice cubes and a lime wedge left in her glass. "Steady now, let's wind this up and get to dinner. I can smell the chicken all the way out here. So Brent was not carrying anything, but he seemed to spring from the bushes near the tavern on his way to get a cup of coffee. It just seemed odd, the way he came shooting out of the bush. And he is leaving town this weekend for the summer break. But since I know he is heir to a spats fortune, I'm not sure what his motivation would be."

"Me neither, and I resent your insinuations regarding my past employment. As you know, I'm completely normal," he said as he stuck out his tongue. "So, let us move young Mr. Wickingham the third down the list, and move us on to dinner."

The smell wafting out of the house drew them by the nose to the kitchen, where they attended to the business of serving themselves dinner. The conversation turned to other topics and the meal was soon finished. Feeling replete, Zeus pushed his chair back and patted his stomach. Maryvonne got up to take the empty dishes away and start cleaning up.

"After I get this all taken care of, I'm going to go on my computer for a while and do some research. We're still planning on going to the festival tomorrow, right? What time?" asked Maryvonne.

"How about around nine-thirty? We should still be able to find a good parking spot by then, and I think the cannons fire at ten." Then he added, "Maryvonne, I want to ask you to be careful about your hunch that the Dunlap Broadside of the Declaration has been stolen. Please don't do anything foolish. I'm pretty sure that in reality this is a non-event, and besides that it seems none of your business. If it's stolen, let the police handle it."

"Have you ever known me to do anything foolish?" she grinned.

"That is what I'm afraid of."

Upstairs at her desk, Maryvonne opened her laptop and set the Pandora to the Jimi Hendrix channel. First song up was the classic Purple Haze. The forceful droning electric guitar immediately dragged her slowly link by link to the top of the rollercoaster, then let go into a drop that gained speed as Jimi's strong voice filled her office.

Purple haze all in my brain
Lately things they don't seem the same
Acting funny, but I don't know why
Excuse me while I kiss the sky

Kiss the airbag is more like it, she thought. *Actually, I wonder if this small bump on my head from the airbag is why I was able to "kiss the sky" and see Tabby? I wonder if I have this ability just for now, or if the channel or whatever it is will close once my swollen bump disappears for good?* Her attention was drawn back to Jimi's voice, and she sat back to enjoy the remainder of the electric roller coaster ride that is Purple Haze.

The song finished and the station went to an ad, so Maryvonne thought about Jimi while his voice still echoed in her head. *What a loss that Jimi died so young and left such a gap. I wonder what other contributions he would have made to the world, both in music and civil rights. He, like Jude Hall, reached for his moment and made a huge success of it. Then the pressure that these two men, centuries apart, must have endured because they both had excelled in a discriminatory white man's world must have been ghastly. It boggles my mind. Mon Dieu! There is no use getting maudlin over it. Let's see what can be done.* And she began typing on her laptop.

Art + Feminism had a website that encouraged her to create a Wikipedia account and add women, femmes, and others into the white, male-dominated online encyclopedia. So Maryvonne did that for a while, adding in small bits of info about the town that could be correctly referenced to Wiki standards. In doing this she inserted a few more of the historical interconnections of Black and white Exeter into the online wiki-world, for all to access. As she typed, the time flew by.

After a couple of hours, she stretched way back in the chair and rested her eyes for a few moments. She then switched gears and spent some time looking up who was already making strides in excavating the historical Black community. The best organization seemed to be the Black Heritage Trail of New Hampshire, based out of nearby Portsmouth. She considered contacting them soon to have a conversation, but felt unsettled about that.

Another thing she thought could be effective was to apply art to the effort. That was more in her comfort zone. Her painting skills would be useful for that, and that could even be fun. Sometimes she did combine art and activism together and created projects that could be called "artivism." But maybe that was what most real art was, anyway.

And lastly, she looked up local genealogists. Perhaps one would like to help to sort out some pieces of this puzzle. She settled on Mr. Krueger, who had just made a local link to a Black man whose heritage traced back to the 272 enslaved Blacks sold by the Jesuits in 1838 to save Georgetown University from financial ruin. He would be perfect. She looked up his phone number and thought about calling him on the phone, but it was getting late.

Rolling her chair back from the desk, she stretched her arms overhead and yawned. She would call him on Monday. The thought then occurred to her that she should check her cell phone now, and catch up on any text messages. Stiffness had crept in from sitting so long in one spot, so she flexed her legs a few times before heading downstairs to retrieve her purse on the counter to check the cell phone. But when she looked in her purse, the phone was not there.

Such a sinking feeling when your phone is not where it should be! Dang! Maryvonne tried to think of where she last saw the phone. She had taken a photo of the hydrangea when she was with Anjali in the pocket park. Had she used it after that? No.

The drink! She had spilled the iced coffee on her shoes and was distracted. She most likely had left her phone on the bench or knocked it off the bench when the drink spilled. She looked at the kitchen clock. It was nine now, and almost dark. But she was going to have to go look for it anyway.

"Zeus, may I borrow your cell phone please?" she called down the cellar steps where he was working in his wood shop. "I think I left mine on a bench downtown, and I could use yours to call mine when I get there and listen to see if I hear it ringing."

"Sure," he replied, "it's on my desk up there. I think the festival kick-off fireworks are going to start soon, so you may be able to see them after you get your phone. Have fun."

In very short order she was steering her electric car silently towards town. She took a long cut to avoid many of the cars parked downtown, and slid soundlessly to a stop on the grass in front of the daycare center, since there was no parking left and she would only be a minute. Through the open car window, she could hear the happy sounds of the festive crowd waiting for the fireworks down by the riverbank in the big grassy area allocated for public viewing. On the opposite side of the car were the darkness of the trees and the small, quiet pocket park.

Clutching Zeus's cell phone, she exited the car, crossed the street and stepped onto the lowest portion of the small brick path. Halfway up the path she stopped to activate the screen and get some light to guide her feet in the dark.

The path rose higher through the river birches and English ivy, which cast strange shadows in the dark. Or maybe she was just getting spooked because she knew there was a very old cemetery just over the rise in the small patch of woods. Despite the heat of the July night, she felt a touch clammy. Now she could see the bench ahead, and the dark path turning left and continuing into the graveyard behind, with its small, bushy opening.

She peered towards that dark, bushy hole; just to convince herself that there was nothing malevolent in that direction. Just as she got to the top of the path and into the clearing, the first firework went off and nearly gave her a heart attack.

It also illuminated the entire area, including the cemetery and its akimbo stones. And there was something else Maryvonne had seen during the flash, and she couldn't believe it. There were two moons out tonight! Of all the times! Clutching the cell phone that she had nearly dropped during the blast she dashed over to the bench and sat down quickly in the dark, hoping the two in the cemetery had not seen her.

The bench was angled so that she could no longer see through the small bushy opening to the graveyard. Which meant that they could not see her either. Maryvonne quickly scanned the bench and didn't see the phone. Looking on the ground she noticed that there was quite a bit of thick English ivy under the bench. She knew that first firework was the warning shot and the next would come in about two minutes and she wanted to find her phone while she could still hear the ring.

Punching the speed dial icon for her name on Zeus' phone, she waited for a ring. It seemed to take forever to connect.

Finally, somewhere in the ivy behind the bench came the muffled jingle of her own phone. She hung up and thrust her hand into the glowing ivy behind the bench, and she immediately felt the shape of the phone. Success! Now how to get out of here without being seen? Boom! The second firework went off, and the third almost simultaneously. The show was on.

Now that the fireworks were going off in full force the dilemma was solved. She would act normal, just look upwards and enjoy the show and pretend she had never seen what she had seen.

But once you see something, you can never un-see it, and when she closed her eyes during an exceptionally bright firework, the vision of it came back to her in all its stark glory. She grimaced, slightly horrified.

Soon enough, Pixie Smithson came hurrying out from the cemetery, flip-flops clicking on the brick path, knee-length sundress swaying in time. Pixie was in the process of smoothing her hair and started slightly when she saw Maryvonne on the bench. Pixie managed a quick hello as she passed Maryvonne and left the park. At a brisk pace she headed up Green Street towards her home on Cass.

When she was out of sight Maryvonne giggled and sat back to wait for the second climax of the night. This one in the sky.

When that initial firework lit up everything Maryvonne had seen the first climax, which involved Brent Wickingham and someone bent over the tomb of Reverend Dudley. Apparently, Pixie was that someone. The good Reverend would have been rolling in his grave.

Chapter 9

Hey Joe
Where you goin' with that bun in your hand?

The next morning, the sun was already promising another hot day as Maryvonne and Zeus drove the convertible to the festival. The long riverfront parkway was closed to cars now for the remainder of the weekend, and a ticket booth was set up at the parkway entrance. After paying for their tickets Maryvonne slipped her tortoise shell sunglasses on, and pulled her visor lower to shield her eyes from the low and bright sun. Maryvonne and Zeus strolled hand in hand along Swasey Parkway wearing matching tee shirts with large American flags and the words "Exeter, Revolutionary Capital of NH" across the front. Maryvonne wore dangling earrings of small flags as well, as an added salute to her country. On her feet were a pair of Portuguese cork wedges in buff. The official opening cannon shot was to be at ten o'clock, but starting at nine early birds could walk the grounds of the simulated military encampments set up by the river.

The morning sun was sparkling in bright yellow streaks off the blueness of the Exeter River. Across the river, the tiny brick Powder House that held all the town's gunpowder back in the 1700's was now guarded by a line of oversized British Redcoat soldier figures that reminded Maryvonne of giant Christmas Nutcrackers. These gargantuan figures could be seen in the distance behind the white canvas tents of the militia "soldiers" and made an interesting juxtaposition between historically accurate and historical kitsch. Zeus got a kick out of it and pointed it out to Maryvonne.

The first part of the grassy parkway where Zeus and Maryvonne stood was now completely taken over by reenactors portraying the American militia who had camped in the canvas tents overnight and were still going through their morning ablutions, including shaving with straight razors and boiling water in iron kettles over small fires. The gargantuan plastic Redcoats seemed to lurk ominously in the woods on the far shore.

For the entire length of the grassy parkway, the next part of the festival was set up with traditional artisans: weavers, pot makers, and even a blacksmith, all dressed in period outfits. It was a colonial artisans village that had been sponsored by the New Hampshire State Council on the Arts. History had truly come alive!

Out of habit, Maryvonne peered at their shoes on the way by. Lots of buckles. She and Zeus planned to walk quickly all the way to the far end of the parkway first, then take their time returning back through to the encampments at the beginning. That way they would be facing away from the low sun. Plus, the food trucks were at the far end, and that was the real first stop for them.

After the artisans came a large enclosed section dedicated to children's games. Past that, in the grassy area where folks had been watching the fireworks last night, a giant beer garden was being set up across from the pavilion stage. A local brewery had pulled up a mobile keg party truck, which was locked and would open at eleven according to a handwritten note taped across the colonial-inspired beer menu. A fiddle band was setting up in the pavilion and Maryvonne noticed a full music schedule posted on both sides of the pavilion. This party was going to go on well into the night.

Further along the parkway, they finally came to the place where the parkway road became lined on both sides with food trucks offering every type of cuisine on the globe. Only one food truck serving breakfast items was open this early. Purchasing two wedges of Johnny Cake streusel, a form of cornbread with a stream of brown sugar and cinnamon running through its core, they moved to a group of picnic tables by the river to eat the crumbling delicacies.

"So, Pixie and Brent, eh?" Zeus smirked as he bit into the cake.

"Oh la la! I'll never forget the expression on his upturned face in the glow of the firework, nor his upturned…" Maryvonne held the cake up to her lips and very salaciously bit into it.

"Ouch!" laughed Zeus, crumbs flying out of his mouth, "and you are sure it was Pixie?"

"Well, it's true, she was bent over the tomb so I did not see her face. I only saw some of her moon - but it was about the right size and shape, and of course, then she walked right by me minutes later. But truthfully, I feel bad for her. Her grandfather abuses her terribly. She deserves to have some fun, so why not?" said Maryvonne, raising her eyebrows and slowly licking the brown sugar off her fingers.

"You are a piece of work, Maryvonne. Now stop that before anyone sees you. Here, take this napkin and wipe your sticky lips," Zeus chided her. "Brent never came out of the cemetery? I suppose he could have exited the opposite direction through the yard of some of the dorms on that side," Zeus theorized, then continued, "I think I heard he lives in the school housing on Governors Lane, that small alley off Spring Street. On a different note, what it does tell me is that Brent is with Pixie... and she works at the IT office, so she has really good tech skills that could extend to hacking into security cameras."

"Yes, and maybe they are in it together, and then Pixie can get away from her mean old Gramps. It's probably time for nursing services anyway. Far past time probably," Maryvonne concluded. "So Brent moves up my list, and I add Pixie too."

They finished their Johnny Cakes looking at the current in the tidal river. Maryvonne made a spiteful show of cleaning the sugar from her lips, then freshened her lipstick. The happy couple headed leisurely back through the festival, which was now starting to really come alive. The Redcoat actors, who were not in tents - since in reality they had been "quartered" in the homes of local folks - were now lining up at the back entrance of the beer garden on the corner of Summer Street, which lay on a hill just outside the parkway grounds. They would soon begin to march in formation into the parkway and commence wandering about, answering questions from attendees, harassing the Minutemen, and sometimes shouting "Long Live the King!"

In the artisan area Zeus was enchanted with the blacksmith, while Maryvonne went to look at the fabrics piled near the looms. What she really wanted to see. though, was "Jude Hall" and his regiment in the encampments. Looking up from the looms she saw the Redcoats marching past her, headed to the encampments. Pulling Zeus by the arm away from the red-hot blacksmith, they followed the soldiers to witness the drama of the first encounter.

But before any of this could happen, a loud voice came over a sound system throughout the whole park and announced it was time for the salute to the flag, and then the national anthem would be sung. There was a large flag being raised over by the river and a small crowd stood near it. A group of school-aged children in costumes led the Pledge of Allegiance, hands over heart, and all adults within hearing distance joined in as well.

When Maryvonne got to the last sentence she was reminded how in grade school she used to recite the pledge, and would silently reword in her head the final line *...and justice for all* into a silly *...and fruit-juice for all.*

Times had changed since grade school and the final line no longer reminded her of fruit juice, but of race relations. Who gets justice, and who doesn't.

The opening strains of the Star-Spangled Banner burst loudly over the whole park and everyone as far as she could see stood still and put their hand over their heart. Even the Redcoats, who were, after all, American actors. In total there must have been about a hundred costumed re-enactors milling about the long parkway and its entrance near the Folsom Tavern. The museum was even selling commemorative tricorn hats and white bonnets so everyone, young and old, could don one and evoke the historical mood.

Over the speakers, a young and lush voice began singing the lyrics. Maryvonne realized it was the young daughter of the Black Pastor of the Exeter Baptist Church. Her mom had power and quality in her singing voice, and it had been announced in the papers that the pastor's daughter would make her singing debut at this year's festival. Hearing this young beautiful voice reminded her of little Rhoda, and how she was asked to sing at a very important and patriotic town event this very day so many summers ago.

Listening to the song with her hand over her heart she thought about how Rhoda married a man who fought for "liberty and justice for all" and then had three of his sons sold into slavery: his and little Rhoda's children. And during that dark chapter of history so were hundreds, if not thousands of others. This was a broken bone in the skeleton of America that had never been set right. Was it better to leave the old injury alone and limp along, or make an intentional fresh break and mend it correctly once and for all, or to seek some variation of healing? She had no answer, sighed, and turned her attention back to the flag. Near the flag was a cannon, and a costumed actor in a tricorn hat was lighting a torch.

The song concluded, and the festival opening was to be officially marked by the firing of a cannon. The fuse was lit and the crowd put their hands over their ears. Boom! What a thundering sound echoing across the whole town! The Redcoats turned and spread out two by two to begin harassing the American militia about taxes, curfews, and more. The festival had begun and the crowd was thickening, family groups meandering while children were running about. Costumed docents were explaining various elements and activities in the encampments.

Wandering about, Zeus and Maryvonne made their way over to the encampment of the mostly Black regiment. A Black soldier was addressing a small crowd gathered before him. He was a tall man who looked exceedingly strong. A wooden musket was strapped to the back of his blue vest, and his cropped knickers showed off his muscular legs. He was introducing himself as Jude, nicknamed "Old Rock," and listing off all the battles he had been involved with.

"The first spring, I was in the 3rd New Hampshire when I got thrown headlong by a cannonball that landed quite close to me at the Battle of Bunker Hill, but that didn't bother me too much. By late summer General Washington said Black men couldn't enlist anymore, but he soon changed his mind. He needed us! So, I enlisted again, this time with the 2nd New Hampshire and over the next three years we went to Ticonderoga, Trenton, and Saratoga, New York and Hubbardton, Vermont. But then I got a little sick, see we didn't have much in the way of warm coats in my company, so I stayed in Albany for a month while my regiment continued on to Valley Forge. Can't believe I missed that one!" He stopped and grinned.

"How did you get the nickname Old Rock?" asked a young boy in the crowd.

"Well, folks also call me Captain. But I'll tell you, son, how I got the name Old Rock. See, I fought at the Battle of Monmouth, and that was one of the toughest fought battles we ever did see. It was when the fighting was all over and we settled down that the company started calling me that name, because they thought I had earned it by my skill and perseverance. After that I served in the Sullivan-Clinton expedition on the southwestern fringes of New York State and was eventually redeployed to guard the Hudson Highlands and the string of forts surrounding West Point." He stopped and took his musket off his back and held it out in front of him.

"This musket did a whole lot of work in those days, but it wasn't over yet. I signed up for one last time. In total I fought for eight years to help America get free from the King and his Redcoats. For my final enlistment, I joined up with the 1st New Hampshire to form the New Hampshire Battalion, and we spent some time down to New Windsor, Connecticut.

When I was finally discharged, I came right back to Exeter. They promised me money for fighting, and don't you know it took a few years but I got it. Right from that yellow house up on the hill there," he pointed towards the Ladd-Gilman house, its yellow color blazing against the blue of the cloudless sky. "Now I am going to marry my sweetheart Rhoda and build us a small house out on Drinkwater Road towards Kensington. We are fixing to have a family soon."

A mixed-race couple had been listening to the talk, and at this point the woman stepped forward and said, "Thank you for your service, Jude." The small crowd murmured in agreement, and then applauded. Maryvonne applauded too; she thought the presentation was nicely done. The actor gave all the pertinent information, but did not appropriate Jude's voice.

Jude took off his tricorn hat and bowed, "You are welcome, and thank you for taking the time to hear my story. It has been a long time ignored." Standing up again to his full, impressive height he smiled and asked, "Any other questions?" A young boy started asking about his musket and Jude let the boy touch the wooden handle while he described it. Maryvonne and Zeus moved on towards the exit.

"I am so glad there was finally a focus on Jude and the Black soldiers' contributions this year. It's a very important part of our history that has been stuffed into the void," Maryvonne said, and Zeus agreed. She added, "They hired the perfect person to represent him. Jude was reported to be a large and strong man which may be why he was such a revered soldier. That guy must be a professional actor, he was excellent."

"Let's see how it goes in the parade today, I think it's at one o'clock. You know, I read that they made the Black veterans walk at the back of the Exeter Fourth of July parades, after all the white soldiers, wearing tattered uniforms. Not very respectful back then in the 1780's and 90's, I hope they change that positioning today," stated Zeus. He took off his baseball cap and wiped the sweat from his brow.

He put his cap back on and continued, "It's almost eleven, let's start to make our way over to the podium on the hill in front of the Ladd-Gilman house to see the horseback rider deliver the Declaration to John Taylor Gilman," Zeus said using his hands to make air quotes for John Taylor. "Who is playing John Taylor this year?"

"Greg Gilman, the banker, he is a direct descendant," Maryvonne replied, her thoughts going back to when she saw John Taylor come bouncing down the very hill the decorated podium was now on, holding his brown hat tight to his head to speak to his cousin Tabitha. Maryvonne had to admit that Greg Gilman did actually resemble him slightly.

They made their way past the stone pillar at the end of the parkway and out onto the sidewalk of the main road. They weaved through the crowd and got a spot with a good view of the podium. At the very front of the crowd stood many small children dressed in period costumes: the girls in long cotton dresses and bonnets, and the boys in waistcoats and breeches. They looked adorable. Redcoats roamed the crowd, jostling the militia who were also beginning to gather. Competing shouts could be heard: "God save the King!" and "No taxation without representation," which was followed by loud huzzahs.

Presently a horse rider did show up and pass off a document, which was ferried up to the podium where Greg, in the guise of John Taylor, was standing along with various costumed representatives of the American Independence Museum. Bella Volpe was the only one in regular clothing. She stepped to the podium in her shiny red Ferragamos and matching red dress with white patch pockets. She fumbled some papers, then spoke into the microphone and welcomed the crowd to the festival, which was in its thirtieth year, and finished by introducing Greg. He stepped forward to address the crowd.

"Ladies and Gentlemen, this very important document has just arrived. Please be quiet while I read it aloud. I am sure we all want to know what it says, it's from our friends in Philadelphia." Greg broke the seal and began to read:

> *IN CONGRESS, JULY 4, 1776*
> *The unanimous Declaration of the thirteen united States of America*
>
> *When in the Course of human events it becomes necessary for one people to dissolve the political bands which have connected them with another and to assume among the powers of the earth, the separate and equal station to which the Laws of Nature and of Nature's God entitle them, a decent respect to the opinions of mankind requires that they should declare the causes which impel them to the separation.*
>
> *We hold these truths to be self-evident, that all men are created equal, that they are endowed by their Creator with certain unalienable Rights, that among these are Life, Liberty and the pursuit of Happiness...*

Greg Gilman, dressed to perfection, was doing the job with aplomb. The crowd was rapt up to this point. Then he launched into a long list of grievances which caused many a shout from the actors in the crowd, as well as the spectators. Maryvonne thought how shocking this speech must have been when it was first read in Exeter by the real John Taylor Gilman in 1776, and wondered what Tabby's reaction to it was. Imagine the thoughts that must have run through her mind. Or that of any slave listening, knowing there was a chance to gain freedom. Or that of the Loyalists in any given family on the verge of a rift already. Who knows who was in the crowd that fateful day when lives were changed forever?

Clearly dripping with sweat now from under his curly wig and tricorn hat, Greg dramatically motioned for the crowd to quiet down, then read the end of the document as the sun blazed on.

> *We, therefore, the Representatives of the united States of America, in General Congress, Assembled, appealing to the Supreme Judge of the world for the rectitude of our intentions, do, in the Name, and by Authority of the good People of these Colonies, solemnly publish and declare, That these united Colonies are, and of Right ought to be Free and Independent States, that they are Absolved from all Allegiance to the British Crown, and that all political connection between them and the State of Great Britain, is and ought to be totally dissolved; and that as Free and Independent States, they have full Power to levy War, conclude Peace, contract Alliances, establish Commerce, and to do all other Acts and Things which Independent States may of right do. — And for the support of this Declaration, with a firm reliance on the protection of Divine Providence, we mutually pledge to each other our Lives, our Fortunes, and our sacred Honor.*

Upon conclusion of the reading, Greg stepped away from the podium, and the crowd cheered, booed, huzzahed, and jumped about with arms flung in the air. A fife and drum band began playing a marching tune. The pandemonium was short-lived due to the heat, and the hot and tired crowd started to disperse, the soldiers heading back their encampments in various moods depending on the color of their jackets, and the people heading to the festival to see the sights and eat lunch and drink beer.

Zeus pulled Maryvonne through the crowd by the arm, "Let's go see the Declaration," he yelled over the crowd. The tavern was very close by and they could see the line at the front door was still small. People entered in a line, passed through the room which held the display, and exited through the back door. It was a thick stream that moved at a steady pace. Maryvonne and Zeus waited in line quietly for a very short time; there was no point in talking, as they both knew why they were there.

Bella Volpe was now working at the table placed outside the entrance at the large granite step. She appeared to be selling memberships to the museum, as well as raffle tickets, at the far end of the table. At the opposite end of the table, closer to Maryvonne, museum volunteers in costume were collecting entrance fees and managing the line.

A dozen people were in line ahead of Maryvonne and Zeus when she saw Bella clumsily knock the entire raffle jar off the table. Luckily it did not break, but the red raffle tickets sprayed out onto the grass. Frantically, Bella knelt and began scooping them up, stuffing them back into the jar. When she stood up, Maryvonne noticed grass stains on her knees and Bella did not. The usually calm and beautiful woman had dark circles under her eyes, and a large chunk of her French twist up-do had fallen out during the scramble. She looked like a woman having a bad day. Maryvonne and Zeus side-eyed each other but said nothing.

When it was their turn, they paid the small donation fee at the table and entered the crowded room in which the document was displayed. A policeman stood guard. It was locked safely inside a large wood and glass hutch on which shone an electric blue light. Small silver stars, hung at various heights, rotated inside the case on very slim wires. The result caused the document to seem to ripple as if it were underwater and alive.

"Tres bon," said Maryvonne, noticing the unusual effect. She looked at the lock. It looked like a double-key sort, similar to a safety deposit box at a bank. She looked at the frame. Nothing stood out. The document inside appeared perfect to her. She and Zeus silently looked around for the security camera, and saw the small glossy ball of a wide-angle lens peeking out discreetly above the case. They were probably being filmed right now, and probably looking suspicious. Maryvonne motioned her head towards the door to indicate that she was ready to leave. They exited the back door in silence, noticing the same type of camera over that door.

Zeus was the first to speak when they finally crossed the street and got well away from the building. They sat on a bench in the same park where Maryvonne had spoken with Anne and Addie the day before. Zeus said, "I didn't notice anything odd about the document, and although I am clearly no professional, the security seemed pretty hard to beat. And I don't know Bella very well; however, I did think that she was acting very anxious. Maybe you really are onto something in your thinking that the document is a fake."

"Not just a figment of my active imagination?" she laughed.

"So, let's run through this again, just in case after the festival is over there comes an announcement that the document really was heisted this weekend. You can file a witness report with the police, maybe there will be a reward."

"Ok. My list is Bella and her employee on the inside job. Then Joe running across the street with his big bag; the framed document could have been in there. Then Brent coming out of the bushes doing who knows what, and planning to leave town tomorrow. He wasn't holding anything, but if he and Pixie are a team, they could get around the cameras." Maryvonne ticked off each suspect on her fingers as she spoke.

"That is a decent list, let's start thinking about what we can do with the reward money," Zeus suggested.

"Mon Dieu! First you don't believe me, my love, now you're spending imaginary money. What a leap!" Maryvonne replied. "Look, if there is a reward, I'll buy you season tickets to the Red Sox. And I'll also buy myself a pile of designer shoes." She laughed and continued, "Now enough with that. Let's go over to Joe Saints and see if Joe is there. And be casual. Be cool. Let's just get some lunch and observe. What's the worst that could happen?"

"Fine. I can be cool. Plus, I'm hungry. Standing in the hot sun listening to Greg read the speech was draining. I need nourishment. And maybe a coffee to pep me up," said Zeus, getting up.

Hand-in-hand they walked past the summer school and into Joe Saints. The old wooden screen door slapped behind them as they entered the air-conditioned cafe. They both breathed the cool air deeply and took off their hats and sunglasses. There was one open table left, so she and Zeus sat down. Maryvonne set her hat and glasses on the table, while Zeus headed to the bathroom.

While waiting for him to return, Maryvonne greeted some friends from her morning coffee klatch who were having lunch at the next table. It was Paula and her young daughter Abigail, who often stopped in for breakfast before school. Abigail attended the Main Street Elementary School and had just finished fourth grade.

After they exchanged greetings Maryvonne said, "Paula, those sandwiches look great. How are they?" She eyed the good-looking sandwiches on their plates.

Abigail piped up, "The sandwiches are really, really good today, Maryvonne. I have the ham and cheese like I always do. No mayo - yuck! Just mustard and pickles. But the bread is different. It's really fluffy and yummy. It's the best sandwich I ever ate here." She then dramatized this point by taking a huge bite.

"Yes, you're right, Abigail," her mother said thoughtfully, "I thought something was different about mine too and now I realize it's the bread. It is both fluffy and crunchy, mmm, just like I like it. Maryvonne, if you are getting a sandwich, ask for it on the baguette today."

"I certainly will!" replied Maryvonne as she got up to join Zeus who was now reading the chalkboard menu over the counter.

Behind the glass counter was the cash register under the "Wall of Shame," an area where the unpaid bills and names of those who dine-and-dash were tacked. To the right of that was an open door that led to the kitchen, over which hung a sign that said "Yankees fans welcome, Red Sox fans please use back door." Joe could be seen through the open door into the kitchen area, his red curls tied back in the red bandana he wore when baking. He appeared to be cleaning up and getting ready to close out his baking efforts for the day. Brenda Sue was at the counter, engaged in conversation with Zeus on his food order.

Maryvonne leaned over the counter and yelled into the kitchen, "Hey Joe, how are you?" Joe looked up and smiled. Wiping his hands on a white cloth, he took a few steps forward and stood in the doorway between the kitchen and the cash register, the Yankees sign just over his head.

"Hi Maryvonne, Zeus, have you been at the festival? It's a hot one out there, but we have air-conditioning in here. Yes sir, we keep our coffee-nest cool," said Joe in a friendly manner.

Zeus had finished placing his order and was watching Maryvonne's conversation quite closely now.

"That's why we came in, Joe. And we are hungry! I saw Paula and Abigail over there eating sandwiches, and I'm going to get myself a ham and cheese too, just like Abigail, with mustard and pickles. She says it's the best sandwich you ever made her. She thinks you have a new baguette recipe. I'd like to try it too." Maryvonne could feel Zeus' eyes move from her to Joe.

She herself was trying to be casual, but she felt like she was staring too intensely. She couldn't imagine being a real detective.

Joe shifted from one foot to the other, and Brenda Sue turned to look at him as well and said, "Yes, Joe, I noticed the bread is different too, a bit crustier on the outside and softer on the inside, is it a new recipe? Some of the customers have commented favorably on it. I was going to ask you about it."

Joe shifted on his feet again. "Do you really think it's that much better?"

"That's the word I hear," replied Brenda Sue.

"Darn old buzzard!" Joe said under his breath.

"What gives?" asked Brenda Sue.

"All right, all right, I confess. I didn't bake those baguettes."

"What on earth?" the surprise was apparent in Brenda Sue's voice.

"I was on the trail of a very elusive bird I want to check off on my life-list at sunrise Thursday morning, and lost track of time. Never happened before. So, I went over to the prep school kitchen in that brick and smoked glass building across the street there." He flung the end of his towel in the general direction. "I had to beg that old buzzard that bakes for them to sell me a dozen baguettes fresh out of his oven. He finally did, and you know what he said? He said he always thought that my baguettes were bland and he predicted that my customers were finally going to have good sandwiches. He bet me twenty dollars." Joe looked very cross.

"Well, I'd say it was twenty dollars well spent. Now you know you gotta change your recipe. You should go thank the guy," replied Brenda Sue, who was somewhat of a kitchen-counter sage.

This caused Joe to brighten as he thought on it. "You might be right," he said.

"Usually am," was her reply.

Maryvonne cleared her voice, to remind them that she and Zeus were still there. "Joe, I saw you the other morning skittering across the street with a big bag, and Hey Joe, I wondered where you were going with that bun in your hand." She giggled as she sang-spoke and the joke flew right over their heads. Except Brenda Sue, who looked at her with laughing eyes and picked up her pen. Apparently, Brenda Sue knew her Jimi Hendrix songs too.

"All right, what would the clever lyricist like to order?" she asked wryly.

"Ham and cheese on baguette please, with mustard and pickles."

"Ok, I'll bring your sandwiches over to your table in a jiffy. How is the painting going? Are you putting anything in the festival's art auction this year?" she asked as she rang up the order.

Now it was Maryvonne's turn to look cross. She had completely forgotten about that! Brenda Sue noticed her turn in mood and looked at her with concern.

"Yes, and you just reminded me about it. I'm painting the Folsom Tavern this year, and it's not quite done. Oh no! I have to finish it quickly, but these crowds are not going to work. Darn it! The parade is starting at one o'clock. I won't even be able to see the tavern until it's too late."

Maryvonne stood there at a loss.

"No problem," said Brenda Sue. She turned and looked at Joe who was still standing there and said, "Front office?" He nodded and disappeared into the kitchen.

Maryvonne blinked.

Brenda Sue laid it out: "There's a room directly above this cafe with two large picture windows that look out directly onto the tavern. It's a one room office, right at the front, and the guy just moved to a larger office in Merrill Block. What do you need, like an hour or two? Joe has a key: he has extra keys to all the offices up there. That way if someone gets locked out, they just come down and get the extra from Joe. Cuts down on locksmith fees. Those people charge a fortune." At that very moment Maryvonne was in love with the divine Miss Brenda Sue.

"Magnifique! You are a wonderful woman! Thank you. May I have the key now? After we eat, I'll go home and get my paints and come right back and won't have to bother you again."

"Sure, I'll get the keys from Joe and bring them over to your table with the sandwiches. There are two keys; one for the office itself, and another for the street-level door in the middle, right next to our entrance."

As he paid for the sandwiches Zeus said, "My old friend from the prep school used to have an office up there off to the left when he was doing research for his book, and I visited once in a while. Upstairs will work out perfectly for you, Maryvonne. Thanks for helping, Brenda Sue, we owe you one."

"Don't mention it," she said and the kitchen-counter sage went in the back to start making the sandwiches.

Chapter 10

Crosstown traffic
All you do is slow me down,
and I'm trying to get on the other side of town

"Mon Dieu! I can't believe the painting slipped my mind! At least there's enough time to put the finishing touches on and have it mostly dry. I did put on the first thick coat of gloss Thursday, so the next coat can be thinner and should set quickly. I'll finish it and then walk it over to the art gallery in the town hall right away." Maryvonne was standing in her kitchen in her painting outfit with her art supplies and equipment in a pile, ready to go.

"How long do you think you are going to be gone?" inquired Zeus.

"Well, traffic is going to be bad because of the George Washington parade at one o'clock, and I'm going to have to park pretty far away and lug all this stuff. But the painting should be finished up in less than an hour. There's really only a small amount left to do, mostly the shading and highlighting. So, I should probably be back in two hours or so."

Zeus yawned, then said, "Ok, I think I'll mow the back lawn and then take a quick nap while you are gone. Enjoy the parade, you're going to have the best seat in the house perched up there painting."

The streetlight at the bottom of High Street went through three cycles before Maryvonne made it past. Traffic crawled through the main street into town and across Great Bridge, which was actually a very small bridge. Maryvonne had her Jimi CD on the player, so she didn't mind the crawling too much. She smiled when the tune Crosstown Traffic ripped through the speakers, and turned it up.

That Jimi had it "going on" for way back then, she thought. *No wonder he was such an icon from early on. He practically invented the sound of the over-amped electric guitar, all that wah wah feedback stuff, and trippy sound moving from the left speaker to the right. Genius! And so fun! And when he headlined Woodstock, what a ripping rendition of the Star- Spangled Banner he performed in that fringed white jacket. Who realized back then he was part Cherokee? A Black Native-American performing an electric outer-space version of the Star-Spangled Banner to thousands of mostly white folks. Totally ironic and iconic.*

Finally across the bridge, she turned left and away from the festival, to skirt around the outside of downtown and move easily to the other side. After skimming down past Long Block and the Bungalow Club, she turned right and came out near the Senior Center. She was still pretty far away and cars were parked all along even these roads. She wanted to get to the north side of town before she started looking for a spot, but this jammed side-street parking did not bode well. Parking would be even worse on the north side now, and the roads would be blocked off because of the parade route.

Deciding to ditch her car soon, she turned left and managed to find a small spot on a corner into which only a tiny Miata like the Zeus-mobile would fit. The noontime sun was shining hotly overhead, and Maryvonne knew this was going to be a hot walk, carrying all her art gear. Clamping her hat on her head, she felt a tingle in the remainder of her flattened bump. *Not bad,* she thought, *this should be the final day of tenderness, and the color is just about normal too.*

She trekked a while in the unrelenting sun and finally made it to the red brick Baptist Church near the center of town. Past the church and off to the right, two small back-to-back parking lots were shaded by a canopy of trees. It was a short-cut that bridged two streets. The second lot faced out onto Center Street, at the corner of Governors Lane near the museum. Knowing the shade would feel good, she cut through them both, hugging near the trees to stay out of the sun. She stepped out onto the sidewalk, but then paused under the shade of a large tree. She had to set her art bags down for a minute to gather energy before she tackled the last leg in the blazing sun.

That would also require walking through the hordes of people lining Water Street waiting for the parade.

Wiping the sweat off her hands and onto her painting smock, she flexed her tired fingers and let them breathe for a minute. The sounds of the festival rippled up the hill towards her. She was approaching the back of the Ladd-Gilman house, and in the distance she could see the sun reflecting off the windshields of all the cars parked in its rear lot. A figure in Colonial garb, looking very smart in a yellow vest and blue breeches, came up over the hill. Maryvonne smiled to see how perfectly situated he looked walking the path alongside the old Ladd-Gilman house. It was like witnessing a time-warp.

The figure quickly crossed the entire parking lot, and as he approached the front walk of the old brick house on the corner of Governors Lane, he took off his brown tricorn hat to wipe the sweat from his forehead. Maryvonne realized it was Brent Wickingham. Hat in hand, Brent turned and dashed up the steps, moving past the white columns and entering the brick house with a bang. Maryvonne stared at the shut door.

Why would Brent be costumed? Maryvonne thought. *He must be a volunteer at the museum. He is a history teacher after all, he would be perfectly suited to it. Now I wonder about him and Bella acting as a team! He actually must have been in that crowd of people with her standing behind Greg Gilman as he read the Declaration. Does he live in this house?* Her eyes searched for a school plaque on the outside, and yes, the school logo of a red dancing griffin was there.

Time was ticking away and she had a painting to finish, she could think more about the implications of this later. She had only minutes to get to the building before the parade blocked her from crossing the street. Picking up her gear again she stepped into the sunlight, and headed downhill towards Joe Saints, threading her way between the jumbles of humanity waiting for the parade to begin.

Tucking into the small paved alcove with three doors at the front of Joe Saints, she was glad to be off the sidewalk and into the shade. Setting her gear down, she fished in her purse for the keys Brenda Sue had given her earlier, found them and unlocked the door. Pulling her gear inside the small landing at the bottom of the stairs, she turned and re-locked the door, then immediately started up the narrow staircase. At the top, she set all the stuff down again with a thud. Whew! She was finally here, what a slog of a journey. She took some time to look around and catch her breath.

The top of the staircase was stuffy and hot, and dimly lit with a small fixture. This was a no-frills office room rental set-up. As her eyes adjusted, she saw two marked doors. One door on the left wall immediately at the landing said "Office 1" with a nameplate in Latin which read "Velocius Quam Asparagi Coquantur." What did that sign mean? Did they import asparagus?

She turned her attention toward a second door directly in front of her that said "Office 2 - Listening Circles." The hall turned sharply to the right past these two doors. Maryvonne stood at the turn and her eyes were drawn to the left. The glowing sunlight fell sharply through the small square window in the back exit door, which was down at the far end of the narrow hallway.

Maryvonne turned the opposite way and saw a door towards the front that read "Office 3" with a "For Rent" sign on it. "Voilà, ici," she said out loud. Taking only her purse and leaving most of her gear where it was, she walked past a small, heavily scuffed half-wall that prevented people from falling down the stairs. She stood in front of the door. Inserting the key, she heard it click and she felt a sense of relief. A very bright room with four picture windows, two in the front and one on each side, greeted her when she opened the door. She was so happy to have finally arrived.

Quickly she went back down the small hallway and retrieved all her gear and brought it inside the room. Shutting the door, she looked around carefully. She loved the room; it was like a glowing white box - it would actually make a perfect art studio. It had great light and was very open. To her delight she saw the west windows showed a clear view of the Folsom Tavern, high above the crowd waiting for the imminent parade.

The room was bare except for a large wooden desk and chair which sat upon a cheap wall-to-wall rug in dark brown. Maryvonne spread out her paint supplies on the desk, and then started setting up her easel just inside the window. Beginning to sweat again, she realized it was too stuffy in the room and looked around for the air-conditioner. It was a new-style heat pump with a remote control. She clicked the button to turn it on and stood in front of it to cool down. She decided that leaving the door ajar would help with the airflow, so she crossed the room and opened it just a few inches.

After placing the painted canvas on the easel and securing it, she studied what she had painted so far. It was good, but she had been interrupted and did not get to the smaller details that give a painting depth and sparkle. Which was actually ok, because she had been painting in the early morning with long shadows, and now it was noon and the sun was casting better shadows in better directions. It would make the painting pop more. Standing right in the window she took a good look at the light and shadows being cast on the house and tree. Yes, she liked it. She felt grateful to be able to use this space; it could actually be marketed as an art studio instead of an office. She made a mental note to mention this to Brenda Sue when she returned the keys.

Looking up and down the crowded street she saw that the automobile marking the start of the parade was just rounding the corner to begin its journey past the tavern and up through the crowd lining the sidewalks. Her timing had been great! Heading the parade was a new model Tesla Roadster convertible in red, in which the marshal of the parade was seated in the passenger seat, giving the royal wave to the crowd. The marshal this year was the first Black regent of the Exeter chapter of the Daughters of the American Revolution, Reisha Raney. The sporty convertible was creeping along very slowly, which Maryvonne thought pretty funny, as she knew the car could do zero-to-sixty in 1.9 seconds, which actually constituted nearly 2G force. She imagined the car zooming down the street like a military fly-over to start the parade. That would get the crowd's notice!

Quite a distance behind the convertible, where the real parade began, she saw a glittering man on a horse and knew it was George Washington. He was resplendent in blue and gold, and wore a very fancy tricorn hat befitting his status as general. A well-dressed fife and drum band marched behind him in exact rows, and beyond that looked to be the militia. Maryvonne waited at the window until the militia got closer. Looking across the street she could see that the line to enter the tavern to see the Declaration was still long. For her painting, she would pretend the crowded line was not on the steps, and instead focus on the elements of the building only. Scanning the workers at the ticket table she saw Bella pass her cash box to a new volunteer, and then slip inside the tavern door.

George Washington had now advanced, and was directly under the picture window, Maryvonne looked past him towards the rows of militia and noticed that Black, brown, and white soldiers all marched together in no particular order. No color line, just people united in a common cause: freedom. "Bon," she said under her breath, and turned to go sit in front of her easel and get to the painting. Time was slipping away.

From her seat she could no longer see the parade progressing under her, only hear it mingled with the hum of the cool air flowing from the heat-pump. She squinted across the street, she was not going to need to bother with her bifocals, she could see the tones and shadows easily enough. Not much detail work was needed today. When her plastic palette board had all the right color blobs on it, plus a dot of Mars Black for the shadows, she started the mental glide to blot out the crowd and soon relaxed into it. Looking up. Looking down. Under the eaves; brown plus black mixed into a dark shadow that slid off her brush and onto the canvas. Under the tree; green and a bit of black. Alongside the granite-slab front step; brown, green and a dash of black swirled on the palette then transferred to the canvas. It was like a dance.

Almost fifteen minutes later she felt finished with the shadows. Looking up a final time she scanned them as a whole, then turned back to the canvas and adjusted the shadows here and there. Finished. There was a long pause in the dance while she cleaned her brushes in her purple cup and readied herself to move on to the highlights. The parade had just finished and the street was resuming a normal level of noise.

Squeezing a blob of Titanium White onto the palette now and spritzing water over the other colorful blobs, she started the brush dancing across a fresh working area of the palette. She found that squinting and softening the focus of her eyes helped her to better see the shapes of the highlights and the negative spaces instead of the objects. Parts of the roof began to be washed with a golden, sun-tinged white, and the leading edge was treated to a splash of dazzling white. Throwing her gaze across the street again she took in the way the sun clung to the top of the maple tree. Green and white blended to ride high atop the tree, with occasional splotches of pure white shiny leaves where the sun reflected strongly.

She chose a smaller brush now - a Bright size two. Squeezing the purple water sprayer again, she spritzed all the colors to moisten them. Starting at the very top of the house and tree, she splashed sunlight onto them. Next level down, her eyes studied the windows. Each window had a splash of dazzling white in the lower right pane. She dipped her brush in pure white and baptized each window on the canvas in front of her with a thick single tiny stroke of white.

Looking further down the front of the house, she noticed that the top of the front door handle shone brightly too, as did the far corner of the granite slab step, just as it turned to the darkest part of its shadow. That is how painting light worked, the brightest next to the darkest to create the illusion of depth. Maryvonne painted those strokes onto her canvas very deliberately.

At last, feeling the painting was finally done, she stood back to survey the completed canvas.

Just then, Maryvonne heard the downstairs door open and then slam shut. The sudden loudness startled her and she whirled around. Someone was entering the building, it seemed to be two people having an argument.

"Don't be mad, it's only for a week or two. I will get everything settled, then you can join me," said the male voice.

"That is such crap, I don't believe you. I've caught you in soooo many lies lately - why should I believe you? What are you up to? I feel like you are using me or something," said an angry female voice.

"That's crazy talk."

"Don't you call me crazy!" yelled the woman.

"Calm down, you know I love you. Let's just go upstairs into my office where it's more private and talk this over."

"This is such bullshit, all you are going to do is lie to me some more," shouted the woman as very loud footsteps began to bang up the stairs. Maryvonne froze, she hoped they were not coming her way.

They didn't. They stopped at the top of the stairs and she heard a key fiddling in the lock of one of the other offices.

Nearer now, the woman began sobbing while speaking, "I was so happy when I saw you coming down the hill with the flowers and the suitcase. So happy. How could you do this to me? Get these goddamn flowers out of my sight." Maryvonne heard a soft swish, which she assumed was a bouquet of flowers hitting the floor and then scuffling noises while the woman half screamed, half cried, "I hate you, I hate you. I hate you!"

"Pixie, relax. You have to believe me. I'm just going on ahead to get things settled. You give your two weeks' notice at work, then come join me. It's better this way, they'll give you a good reference. I'll rent us a place and have it all ready when you arrive. Now come inside and let's work out the details before you give me a ride to the train station. I promise it'll be alright. I love you." Pixie gave a small sob in reply.

Pixie? Was this Pixie being jilted by Brent? Maryvonne thought to herself. The voices of the couple moved further away. Maryvonne took a quick peek out her door into the hall. The door to the asparagus office was half open and the landing was bare except for a large black leather rolling suitcase with a scraggly white ribbon tied to the handle, and a half-trampled bouquet of red, white, and blue flowers. This gave Maryvonne a sudden idea.

Moving quietly into the hallway, Maryvonne ducked down, using the half-wall to shield her movements. Peeking out from down low behind the wall, she saw Pixie and Brent seated on a couch inside the small office, which was not much of an office, more like a love nest. Brent had his arms around Pixie's sobbing shoulders, and his forehead on hers. The black suitcase in the hallway sat quite close to Maryvonne, in a puddle of flower petals and stems.

Reaching out only her hand from behind the wall, Maryvonne slowly rolled the suitcase towards her and behind the wall. She just wanted to have a quick peek inside. Wasn't that what Tabby was trying to tell her to do?

The crying had subsided inside the office, but she could still hear that they were animatedly talking. Maryvonne gently lowered the big suitcase flat on the floor, and listened again. Still talking. As quietly as possible she began to unzip the zipper, and stopped halfway. Still talking. She unzipped it all the way. Still talking. She opened the top with one hand and used the other to fish around inside. It was tightly packed. At the bottom she felt...what? Bubble wrap?

Using both hands she dug to the bottom to try to extricate the thing in bubble wrap. It was large and flat, nearly the size of the suitcase. *Mon Dieu, this cannot be what I think it is.* She gave up trying to pull it out carefully from under the clothes and took hold of a whole pile of clothes and shoes and underwear and threw it on the hallway floor.

Now she could see it. Pulling back a corner of the bubble wrap sleeve, she gasped. Yes, it was indeed what she thought it was!

Without thinking she picked up the large frame, still bubble-wrapped, and bolted towards the steps, nearly tripping on the mashed flowers spewed on the floor. Brent came flying out of the door with Pixie right behind him.

"Give me that back!" he yelled menacingly and lunged at Maryvonne. She just made it past him and onto the first few steps with him right on her heels.

"What the hell is going on?" sobbed Pixie, now standing alone at the top of the stairs clutching her purse to her chest in fright.

Maryvonne was halfway down the stairs now, and Brent caught her by the hair and jerked her head back. This caused both Maryvonne and Pixie to screech. Brent used his other hand to pull on the frame, at which point the bubble wrap was ripped from the frame and the stolen Declaration was completely exposed under the glass.

Pixie yelled out, "You bastard, I knew it!" and threw her purse down the stairs hitting Brent square in the back of the head. The impact caused him to wobble forward and backwards and lose his grip on both Maryvonne's hair and the frame.

Free, Maryvonne ran down towards the door, dragging the frame behind her, step for step.

At the door now, she pushed on the bar and the door flew open, but Brent was too fast and had his hand on the end of the frame again and pulled hard, causing Maryvonne to lurch backwards, still holding a firm grip on the frame. Pixie was still screaming at the top of the stairs.

This commotion at the open doorway caused a couple of passing Redcoats to stop and stare. Then they stepped forward quickly and fixed their bayonets towards the scuffle.

"*Both of you, stop right there!*" they commanded loudly. Maryvonne and Brent both looked up at the Redcoats and froze at the same time, even Pixie stopped screaming. A few curious passersby stopped to stare at the spectacle.

Brent turned and shot back up the stairs like a cannonball. Pixie now began yelling, "You are so screwed you bastard!" Maryvonne looked up the stairs and saw Brent push Pixie over inside the office doorway on the way by as he rushed down the narrow hallway towards the back exit.

On her knees at the bottom of the stairs, Maryvonne returned her stunned gaze to the bayonets still pointed at her. The confused soldiers were still gaping at the scene at the top of the stairs. They finally relaxed, put their guns down and helped her up. Maryvonne clutched the frame to her and shakily addressed the Redcoats.

"Would one of you get a police officer, and the other one stay here with me?" They immediately complied. As one soldier turned away and ran up the street, Maryvonne and the soldier who stayed to guard her went back inside to the staircase and shut the outer door. The small crowd that had gathered on the sidewalk began to disperse.

Pixie was seated dejectedly at the top of the stairs in a pile of petals with her head in her hands, crying softly to herself. Within moments, a police officer appeared at the door and came in, attended by the Redcoat.

"What is going on here?" he asked in a commanding tone, taking in the sweeping sight of Pixie, the mashed flowers and shredded bubble-wrap streaming down the staircase, and Maryvonne at the bottom holding the back of her head where Brent had ripped out some hair.

"Please, officer, come upstairs where we can all talk privately," said Maryvonne, not sure what she was even going to say. "And Redcoat guys, please come too. You are important witnesses. Thank you for stepping in."

Trooping up the stairs and past all the spewn clothes and the open suitcase, the group came into the front office with the easel. Maryvonne didn't bother to shut the door. The officer listened carefully while she described some, but not all, of what had happened. About halfway through her story he paused her, and called on his radio for back-up to come up to the offices above Joe Saints.

There was an awkward silence in the room while they waited for the second officer to arrive. The Redcoats looked out the window at the panorama of the festival spread out below them. Pixie stood alternately sniffing and scowling in a corner. Maryvonne studied her painting, and the officer studied them all. Two other officers arrived and Maryvonne began the story over from the beginning and continued through to the end.

"But why did you think it was in his suitcase?" the first officer, who turned out to be a Lieutenant, questioned.

"Because I overheard a conversation between two employees of the museum, and I had seen Brent looking suspicious that morning. I think you should get the director, Bella Volpe, to come over here. She must be working inside the tavern right now." Maryvonne had decided to keep Tabby out of this.

"Perhaps, but first I want to ask Pixie a few questions," he replied staunchly and fixed his gaze on the purple-haired girl. "Pixie, why don't you tell me what you know about it?"

Pixie raised her weepy face and looked at him sadly. "I don't know much about it. I was surprised to see the Declaration on the stairs, but I knew what it was right away. Brent and I have been dating for about six months now. I always had this niggling feeling that he was using me somehow... and now I understand." At this, the tears came back for a moment and then stopped.

She went on, "He lived in school housing and I live with my gramps, so Brent rented that office over there for us to be together on breaks and things. We would meet there often in the day, sometimes at night. He told his boss he had rented it to work on his antique shoe book. On many of our dates he would ask that I bring my laptop over too, he said he loved to see my hacking skills in action." Here she paused for a sarcastic laugh, ran her hands through her purple spiky hair, then the look on her face turned very dark.

"I see now that he duped me, that he was just using me. I was so desperate to get away from my mean old grampa, and he knew it. I'm at my wit's end. Brent told me we were going to leave town and start a new life together in Hawaii. He was going to work at the prep school there, and I can work online from anywhere. Damn! I just fell right into his trap! What a jerk I am! What a jerk he is!"

Maryvonne thought Pixie looked quite angry now, and was glad, for there is nothing like a woman scorned to help mend a broken heart quickly.

"Please continue, Pixie," said the Lieutenant.

"Well, he especially liked to see me hack into cameras. We would watch all sorts of private cameras like it was a television show. It gave me the creeps, but he loved it, he would laugh and mock. I should have known right then he was no good and dumped him. Damn! Sometimes he would ask me to interrupt the feed or freeze the image on the output, just to play with the minds of the owners. We would schedule times for the live feed to go off and on like it was haunted - he got such a kick out of that. I figured there was no harm in a fifteen-minute black-out on a random schedule. He had a whole list of cameras. I was able to hack into them all, mostly."

Almost as an afterthought she said softly, "And yes, I was able to hack into the ones across the street. I suppose I'm an accomplice," she lowered her head in shame.

She composed herself then continued, "You have to believe me; I had no idea what he was up to. He volunteered over there as a historical docent. I thought the camera view was pretty boring compared with other cameras he asked me to hack. But I had the feeling something was up, though I thought it had to do with Bella. He seemed to have eyes for her. I admit I felt jealous of little Miss Red Shoes. Ugh. Brent must have manipulated the times of the museum cameras' black-outs on the code screen while I was not looking. See, I would often fall asleep after…" Pixie turned red and looked angrier than ever.

The police officer cleared his throat, "I do see. But so far, we do not have solid evidence that there has been a crime committed in regards to this document on the desk. This allegedly stolen Declaration must be verified."

The Lieutenant asked the female officer, whose name was Bailey, to go across the street and find Bella and bring her to this room. The Lieutenant and his backup stood close by the frame, which lay on the desk beside Maryvonne's painting palette and cleaning rags.

Again, the group in the office milled around in awkward silence while Bella was fetched. Standing silently at the windows on high, they saw her walking towards Joe Saints with Officer Bailey.

The disheveled Bella was still a hot mess in hot shoes when she entered the office ahead of Officer Bailey with a questioning look on her face, and faded grass stains still on her knees. She scanned the odd group assembled in the room; policemen, Redcoats, a girl with purple spiky hair and Maryvonne in an art smock.

"What can I do for you…?" she began, but her voice trailed off as her eyes left the faces and roved across the desk. She flew over to the frame and picked it up and inspected the lower left corner of the metal part of the frame. "Oh my God!" she whispered and fell to her knees, still holding the frame in her hands. Then she kissed it.

"Bella, can you identify this?" the Lieutenant asked.

Rising to her feet again, she gently placed the document on the desk and turned to face him. "Yes. It's the museum's original copy of the Dunlap Broadside of the Declaration of Independence," she said, with a big smile on her face. She was positively glowing. "Why is it here?"

"I'll ask the questions, Bella. Everyone, down at the station." He turned to the other officer, "But first, Mike, go out the back door and get on the trail of Mr. Wickingham. Sharp eyes now. And Bailey, please escort this group to the police station for depositions. I'll stay and secure this scene until the detectives get here."

Everyone seemed glad to finally be released from the room, except Bella, who looked anxiously over her shoulder at the Declaration on the table and said, "You will keep a good eye on it, won't you Lieutenant?"

"That's what we do, ma'am," he replied, unhooking his radio and getting ready for crime scene protocol.

"Lieutenant, please," said Maryvonne, "may I bring my painting to the town hall gallery on the way by? It's due there right now for the Festival's art auction tomorrow. I will just hand it off to someone else to hang. It won't even take thirty seconds." He paused for a moment, then agreed.

She took the painting off the easel and placed it on the desk then quickly signed her signature with a paint pen as the others were filing out the door. She left all her art supplies as they were and, holding the painting gingerly in two hands, went into the hall where the others were waiting with Officer Bailey, amongst the suitcase debris.

Chapter 11

Are you experienced?
Have you ever been experienced?
Well, I have

Standing in the soft grass, Maryvonne pushed her shovel into the soil in front of Tabby's grave. More than a week had passed since the incident at the Exeter tavern, and Maryvonne had immediately been cleared of any wrongdoing. In fact, she was now somewhat of a celebrity around town.

Yes, Brent had actually done it, and he was still on the run. The real fifteen minutes of footage from the two cameras was retrieved showing him unlocking the case at five forty-five Thursday morning with secretly copied keys. He replaced the framed document with a pretty convincing fake he had brought with him wrapped in kid's birthday wrapping paper, and then tucked the bubble-wrapped authentic framed document under the cut sod outside near the back door and put the flower pot on the top to keep people from walking on it. A second fifteen-minute's worth of missing footage from the following evening at six-thirty showed Brent at the sod with a very large cardboard box, which had a false bottom, into which he slipped the frame while pretending to tighten the laces on his faux Chuck Taylor sneakers. Apparently, he had then audaciously carried the stolen Declaration into the bookstore with him for his author talk that night.

Bella was also cleared of any wrongdoing. When Spencer had shown Bella the frame, she also had a strong feeling that there was a problem, but did not want to admit it. They both were familiar with the small scratch on the bottom left of the metal frame of the real document. Bella thought it resembled an airplane, Spencer said dog bone. Either way, she knew something was probably amiss but Bella did not want to upset the festival. She planned to report it the morning after the festival, but was a wreck over that decision.

And young Pixie had been duped indeed. She was also cleared, receiving only a slap on the wrist for hacking. Whispers around town said that she had agreed to lend her hacking skills to the police department on secret occasions, and that led to some agreement that enabled her to keep her job at the IT department. And happily, the police had referred social services to her case and they got her grandfather professional nursing help. Which gramps hated. But Pixie loved.

Maryvonne was pretty closed-mouth about Tabby to the police and public; only Zeus knew, yet he did not believe. Regardless, in gratitude she had decided to seek out Tabby's grave and plant some flowers. The Brim had mentioned that both Tabby and Jude's graves were in the Winter Street Cemetery.

The trunk of her hybrid car held a shovel, two large red geraniums and various small pots of white alyssum and blue Forget-Me-Nots. Maryvonne slid her car silently into the dirt parking area outside the old cemetery gate. Tabby's white tombstone had been easy to find over towards the adjacent playground. But it was hard to read, it was so eroded. After wiping it for a while, Maryvonne finally made out these etched words:

In memory of
TABITHA
relict of
Hon. Samuel Tenney
who died
May 2, 1837
Aged 75
Beloved and lamented
She is not dead, just sleeping

Ha! Just sleeping, indeed. I wonder if I'll ever see her again? Maryvonne thought. Tabby's thin white headstone was a perfect match to her husband Samuel's. The childless couple rested side-by-side, overlooking the playground where children were enjoying themselves, laughing and running. The graveyard almost seemed a happy place with sounds of the children playing nearby.

Maryvonne finished digging out a small patch of grass from in front of Tabby's stone in order to make space for the flowers. She pushed in the red geranium, and surrounded it with the blue and white smaller flowers. Clapping the loose dirt off her garden gloves, she stood up and surveyed her work.

Grounding herself with slow breath, she picked up the jug of water she had brought with her and slowly began to water the flowers. As she poured the water she said aloud, "Merci beaucoup, my sister Blue Stocking. On behalf of all feminists, I thank you for your writings, your bravery and your cleverness. And on behalf of myself, I thank you for allowing me to see you and the shadows of things that have gone before. I do hope I was worthy of your effort to reach me. Namaste."

She set down the empty jug and reverently gave a slow bow with her hands clasped at her heart. Then she gave the fem-eye, and laughed.

Exiting the cemetery through the iron gate, she returned the empty pots to her car and got the flowers intended for Jude.

She headed toward a spot exactly opposite Tabby's stone, closer to the train tracks. On the far outer edge a large grey memorial stone had been erected in 2000 by a man who was a descendant of the farmer who had enslaved Jude, since Jude's actual grave could no longer be located in the cemetery. On the large memorial stone were etched these words:

JUDE HALL
born ca 1760
Slave of Philemon Blake
Of Kensington

Fought in the Battle of Bunker Hill
Served til the end of the Revolutionary War, 1783

Married Rhoda Paul 1786
Lived as a free man on
Drinkwater Road, Exeter

Died ca 1827
Buried in this yard

This stone erected A.D. 2000

As Maryvonne pushed her foot on the shovel edge and began to dig out the matted grass to clear an opening for flowers, she thought how Rhoda must have stood searingly bereft somewhere in this grassy area so long ago. Her husband dead, only one son left - the other three stolen, apparently the neighbors didn't care. No wonder she moved far away from this town, the only place she had ever lived, to be with her daughters in Belfast.

Maryvonne put the shovel aside and gazed with melancholy at the blank dirt space she had created, until she remembered that was only part of the story.

As she placed the flowers in their soft holes, she thought how the one remaining son, George, had been helped by the town in a way, and later his son, Moses Hall, was one of the very first Blacks to attend the prep school. That was something of a redress. Yet, it did not seem enough.

Something was still missing; even after two hundred years, the abscess was still apparent.

But again, she had no answers. Sighing, she poured the water on Jude's flowers. She silently thanked him for his contribution to the founding of this country, his leadership and his bravery. She wondered what the genealogical report would reveal.

But for Rhoda, Maryvonne had nothing to say right then. Another day she would go to the scene of the crime, the pond on Drinkwater Road, and see the water which had borne witness and washed tears. Maryvonne wanted to say she was sorry while standing on that very spot of ground.

Collecting the empty pots and shovel, she loaded them into the car and with heavy heart made her way across town to return home and see her husband and her dog.

The big, fluffy dog greeted her at the door and Zeus was in the kitchen squeezing limes when she arrived. "Surprise cocktail hour! I am making you a cocktail," he said, "so meet me on the swing in five minutes to celebrate."

"Celebrate what?"

"It's a surprise, now go wash up and meet me out there," he chided her.

"Yes mon chéri. Toute de suite!" She ran upstairs to wash her hands and fix her hair, glad to be home with her husband. He was always upbeat. She loved that about him. And the dog was always enthusiastic too. As she brushed her hair in the mirror, she thought about how dogs tend to resemble their owners, and smiled. What a pair they were.

Maryvonne was gently rocking herself on the swing and admiring the red roses, when Zeus came out with the two Tequila-Lime Fizz drinks. She stopped the motion so he could sit down without spilling the drinks. He handed one to her and raised his glass to clink hers.

"Cheers!" they said at the same time. The fizz tickled her nose when she drank the first sip, she almost sneezed.

"Tell me the news, you have me wondering," Maryvonne said, wrinkling her nose away from the sparkling fizz, but loving its fresh lime-ness all the same.

Those fizzy diamonds bursting and sparkling in the summer sun never got old.

"Mr. Wickingham the third has been apprehended. He did manage to make it to Hawaii under an alias. Apparently, the spats fortune had dwindled drastically, and he was broke but didn't want to deign to work an actual job. He was picked up living in the underbrush on a beach south of the Na Pali coast of Kauai with a bunch of other lost surfer boys who dwell there off-grid. There was a police raid on the surfer boys due to a rash of local coconut thefts, and our Brent just happened to be in the wrong place at the wrong time."

"Coconuts? Ha!" She laughed out loud. "Well, the truth will always out. One way or another."

"It tends that way," said Zeus, grinning and pushing off with his foot to set the swing in soft motion.

As they swung side-by-side, Maryvonne's attention was drawn to a busy bee working on the roses, while *...and justice for all* spangled lightly through her head.

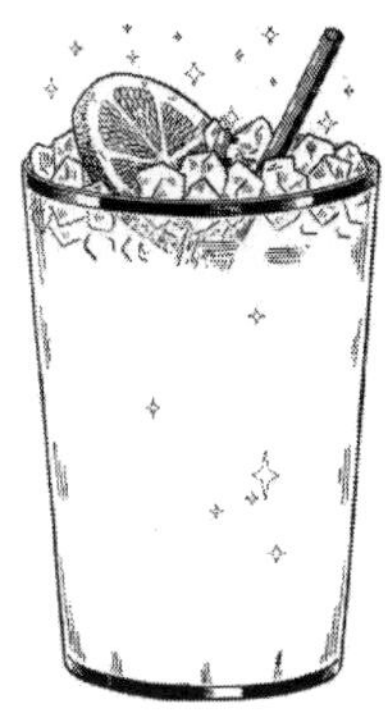

Zeus' Tequila-Lime Fizz

Tall glass
Two tablespoons of frozen Lime-aid concentrate
One shot tequila
One half fresh lime, squeezed
Stir
Add soda water/seltzer
Add crushed ice, and a lime garnish
~Bring out into the sunshine and watch the fizz!

ABOUT THE AUTHOR

RM Allen is an artivist who spends most of her time in New Hampshire with her wonderful husband, whom she adores. She also enjoys looking at shoes.

Read her blog at RM-Allen.com

Books by RM Allen

~~~

Incident at Exeter Tavern
Incident at Ioka
Incident at Exeter Depot

All profits from this series donated to Black Heritage projects in Exeter, NH
~~~

Made in the USA
Monee, IL
21 November 2021

82515142R00092